THE NEXT TIME I BLINK

THE NEXT TIME I BLINK

HEATHER MIHOK

HM Books

For anyone with a shadow on their back.

CONTENT NOTE

This book speaks openly about anxiety and depression. Within these pages you'll find content dealing with topics some readers may find sensitive, such as: mental health, weight and weight loss, suicide, a mass shooting, and the loss of a parent.
If this subject matter is too distressing, please remember you can close this book at any time and find something else to read. It's also okay to seek help if needed. You have the right to protect your peace, now and always.

CHAPTER 1

WHERE AM I? I rub my hands on the ground, cold dirt gathering beneath my fingers. What feels like crisp, scratchy grass tickles my neck. Crickets chirrup in the distance.

Not again. I shouldn't be surprised anymore, but it shocks me all the same.

My eyes won't open. The skin of my lids stick together like superglue. Peeling them apart takes serious effort, and I immediately regret it as bright light pierces my retinas, obscuring my vision. I close my eyes again.

I'd been dreaming, I think. Of something nice, tantalizing, even. A fuzzy, golden warmth just beyond my grasp. Whether it was a puppy, or a comforting bowl of soup, or simply the promise of a peaceful day, I don't know. But my heart glowed with anticipation. I reached for it, stretched my arms to touch it... only I can't remember now.

We're not big on locking doors inside the house. There's usually no need. But tonight, I flicked the lock to my bedroom door. I honestly thought it would keep me there. A small thing – if it had worked, then I'd feel stupid for not trying it sooner.

It didn't work.

I tentatively crack open my eyes. The light comes from a lamp-post above me. Beyond it, the sky is dark as spilled ink. Headstones mark the path I'm lying on, shadowy rows lining both sides.

I'm in a cemetery.

I sit up, slowly, as my head swims with the realization. That's new. I've never woken up in a cemetery. A quick assessment reveals I'm still wearing the same flannel pajama bottoms and oversized T-shirt I went to bed in. But I'm barefoot like the other times, my feet squeaky clean. I don't know how this is happening. It's not sleepwalking. My feet would be filthy and gross, right?

The thing about finding my way home is that I should be navigationally challenged. Without my phone (because it's never on me during these weird blackouts), I don't have access to maps. Yet somehow my feet know which way to go. Of all of this, that's the one silver lining. No need to think, just start walking, and it's like a magnetic force gently pulls me in the right direction. An invisible fishhook through my navel, tugging me home. But that tug can't tell me how far we have to go, or how long it will take, or what we will run into on the way. It's dark, as always, and I wish I had the flashlight on my phone.

Without a jacket, my nerves fire against the October cold, prickling beneath my skin. My senses on high alert, I'm aware of a presence nearby. I can't see it, but I feel it. Is it an animal? A dog, lost and looking for home, just like me? The wind in the trees? A late-night mourner, come to cry over a lost loved one? My bones know, deep down to the marrow, that it is none of these things. Like a heaviness in the air that signals a coming storm, something's off.

I pick up speed, walking at a faster clip. Whatever this is will not stay in the cemetery. It will follow me home.

It always does.

I don't know why it picked me to torture, but here we are, playing a macabre game of hide-and-seek tag. Not my favorite. I didn't sign up for this. And I can't figure out how to make it stop.

I just need to get home.

Ragged breathing behind me sends a chill down my neck. I glance over my shoulder to see a guy in too-short running shorts, neon yellow, and a heavy-duty cold weather coat. "Excuse," he puffs, his headlamp bouncing a bright light on the packed-dirt path. He jogs past and I freeze, anxiety clutching my muscles and stiffening my limbs. I watch as he grows small with distance, eventually becoming a bright dot that turns a corner and disappears behind the headstones. Why he's running among graves in the dark is beyond me. Doesn't he feel the danger lurking around us, slinking between the headstones, following in our direction? Guess not. I tell you, all the weirdos come out at night.

So then, what does that make me?

I flinch as I hear a *snap* behind me and move again, faster. In the darkness, twigs crack in surround sound, but I can't see what's causing it. Picking up the pace, I break into a run.

Snap, snap, snap.

Damn it. My arms pump by my sides like a piston, rushing blood faster into my limbs for maximum power. I need to get out of here.

The hair on the back of my neck lifts with a prickling sensation, and not from the cold; it's as if the follicles are reaching out to whatever is stalking me. I see a wrought-iron gate ahead and streetlights illuminating the flat, smooth sidewalk beyond it. Maybe if I get to the light, the thing will hold off long enough for me to catch my breath. That's what happened last time. A neighbor's motion sensor light went off, swathing me in a cool-toned spotlight, and the rustling stopped. But only when I was in the light. Now, I seek it out, hoping for a repeat of that experience.

A cluster of roots catch my feet and I trip, landing hard on my side. "OW." My right hip hits the ground the hardest, and I'm sure it'll bruise. But that's the least of my worries. I'm now a sitting target – literally. Rolling onto my hands and knees, I push myself to a kneeling position, bracing myself to stand. The thing's intentions stretch toward me, a shadowy, invisible tentacle. I can only imagine it wants to hurt me. How and why is still unanswered, but does it really matter? I get up and start jogging toward the gate, wincing. Each step kills my hip, but I push through the pain and continue.

The gate is only a few feet away when I hear a growl, low and inhuman. It came from my left. I want to look but don't stop. *Focus*, I think. *Keep your eye on the prize.*

The prize being home and staying alive.

The gate creaks as I grip the iron bars, chilled with night, and shove it open. Passing through brings a momentary sense of relief, but it's short-lived because I know *it* will follow. I stop for half a second, only to gulp some air and massage the stitch in my side. Then I'm off again, my feet turning in the direction I need to go, even though I don't recognize my surroundings. There's a park immediately to my right, with stubby lampposts lighting up a children's playground, spooky at this late hour, abandoned swings creaking in the breeze. Across the street on my left is a strip mall, closed and windows dark – there are no people here. I'm equally disappointed and relieved. No one to help me if I get hurt, but also no one to hurt me if I get help. No one to commit me if they find out I'm running from something I've never seen.

As predicted, it slows down in the light, a frustrated growl fading into the backdrop of darkness, so I keep near the street-lamps. I can walk normally, as long as I don't stop. I massage my wrist as I walk, eyes darting left and right, hoping to catch sight of my assailant. My wrist throbs with a powerful ache where I tripped. It might be sprained, but I'll worry about it later. A sprained wrist would be the least of my problems. My reflection looks back at me in the darkened glass of the storefronts, the streetlights casting eerie shadows across my face. Just behind my reflection, like my shadow has taken on a life of its own, inside the empty store something moves. I quicken my pace once more.

Finally, after what feels like half the night, my neighborhood comes into view. Little square houses of the picket fence variety line my quiet street, and hope, warm and delightful, swells inside my chest.

Home shines like a beacon in the night, all the lights left on. I don't remember leaving them on, but I'm glad I did. The thing gathers behind me, sensing we're down to the final minutes of our pursuit. I can feel it, thick like spilled maple syrup pooling into a puddle that flows faster and faster as it grows. I break into a full run across the street and hop over the decorative garden stones leading to the steps of the front porch. There's a key buried next to the steps, marked by a small, ceramic frog I once made as a kid. The welcome mat is too obvious to keep it under, as well as on top of the porch light. Those spots are too easy for an intruder to find. We used to keep it there, and it wasn't until the house was breached that I realized how stupid it was. So now it's deep in the earth. It takes some effort digging it up, but it's worth it for peace of mind.

Key in hand, I push open the red-painted door with my full weight. Immediately the sense of terror dissipates, as if I passed through an invisible force field, but I slam it behind me anyway, gasping for breath.

I peek out the window, making sure nothing waits in the yard, but there never is. I lean back against the wood and close my eyes. My skin's hot and damp with sweat, despite the cold outside. I can't feel it anymore, but that doesn't mean it's not still out there, lurking. I toy with the idea of stepping back outside to see what happens, but let's be real. That's something I will never do. Why tempt fate?

CHAPTER 2

WHEN I WAS TEN, I told my parents I was old enough to stay home alone. I'm an only child, so hovering was their passion. Everywhere I went, they went too, be it a playdate, a dance class, or even just bike riding in the neighborhood. One of them would sit on the front porch, coffee in hand, watching to ensure my safety. I looked forward to the day when they'd let me hold down the fort on my own.

They finally agreed to go out for a quick errand or two. No big deal, right? But I was so excited – I had the house to myself for, like, a whole hour! I turned on some music and raised the volume, like I'd imagined cool, older teenagers doing, and danced around the living room. I was stiff and awkward at first because, come on. When had I ever had the chance to let loose like that? It was weird knowing that I wasn't being watched. I could, in theory, do whatever I wanted, and no one would ever know. The mirror by the front door beckoned – a big heavy thing with an ornate brass frame that made it look expensive but really Mom got it on sale at Walmart.

She was always checking her reflection before leaving the house, back when she was thinner, wiping away a smear of lipstick or smoothing a flyaway hair. I leaned close to the glass and examined my face carefully – scrunching my pug nose into a serious expression, peach eyebrows lifting in a semblance of surprise – before sticking out my tongue. I pulled back and looked around, embarrassed. No one saw. No one knew. I could be as dorky and silly as I wanted. So I pulled a few more faces in the mirror and giggled at my reflection.

The front door rattled, and my breath hitched. They were back? Already? Disappointment washed over me, dragging me back to reality. They'd tell me to turn the music down, to be careful dancing around so I don't break anything...or worse, announce bedtime. I rushed to turn off the music and walked calmly back to greet them as if I hadn't been making a fool of myself.

The doorknob wiggled as if they were struggling to get in. They had a key so it should only take a second to open. What was the holdup?

The handle continued rattling, and a sinking feeling pushed my stomach to my knees. What if it wasn't them?

SLAM. The whole plank vibrated from an external force, and my body clenched.

SLAM.

SLAM-SLAM-SLAM.

Someone banged on the door with what sounded like an open palm. Who would do that? Not my parents. Breath hissed between my teeth, and I slowly stepped back, hoping my feet didn't make the floor creak. I didn't know what to do. Call Mom and Dad? Or was this emergency enough for 911?

I watched the door. The vertical windows on either side are frosted glass, so I couldn't see who it was and, hopefully, vice versa. A figure leaned into the window frame. I could make out the blurry shape of a torso, shoulders, neck, and head. The porch light wasn't on. I wanted to turn it on so badly but then they'd definitely know I was home, and I couldn't have that. Whoever it was brought their hands up to the glass, cupping their shadowy face to see. I pressed myself against the wall and crouched, holding my breath in case they could hear the air whistling from my lungs. I pulled out my cell phone – the kid-friendly one "for emergencies only" with parent-approved apps – and readied Mom's number.

"THAT'S MY HOUSE," the stranger bellowed. "GET OUT OF MY HOUSE. WHAT ARE YOU DOING IN THERE ANYWAY?"

My bladder threatened release at his booming voice. Part of me wanted to shout back that this was *my* house, but I feared that taking a stand would make the situation a hundred times worse. I silenced my whimpers with a trembling hand. He continued pounding on the door until I was sure it would break.

I called Mom.

"What's wrong, sweetie?"

I whispered.

"What? I can't hear you. Speak up."

"Mommy?" My voice warbled. "Mommy, come back."

"Why? What's the matter?"

The banging continued. "I'M GONNA GET YOU FOR THIS!"

"Turn down the TV, honey."

"There's a weird person outside." Hot tears slid over my cheeks and dangled from my jaw. "I'm scared."

That did the trick. Her voice took on a firm, no nonsense tone. "We're on our way. Sit tight. The door is locked?"

I nodded, forgetting she couldn't see me.

"Katherine? Is the front door locked?"

"What's happening?" Dad's voice carried through the phone, smaller, indirect. Mom shushed him before directing him to turn the car around.

"Uh-huh," I said.

"Okay, don't hang up. We'll be there in a minute."

It felt like an hour. By the time they got home, rushed and flustered, the man was gone. He just stopped and left. I was too scared to check for him. My parents searched the property and found nothing. Mom made warm milk with vanilla to calm me while Dad left to check with the next-door neighbors.

I was slurping the dregs of my milk when Dad returned. "Did you find anything?" Mom asked.

"It must've been a drunk," Dad said. I kind of understood what that meant, but not totally. "Must've just...lost his way. Neighbors said he was banging on their doors too. The Smiths called the cops, but he's long gone now." I was weirdly happy to hear others had experienced the same thing, that it wasn't my overactive imagination. It validated my fear.

Mom hugged me. "Well, you're okay, and I'm so glad you called. He's gone now, and you're fine. Safe and sound."

Was I really?

After that, I hated it whenever they both left the house, so much that I'd scream, kick furniture, and pull out my hair. I'd cling to their legs, bawling. Nothing could soothe me, and they eventually stopped trying. I'm not proud of my breakdowns, but it worked. They took errands in turn. I had babysitters well past the age of social acceptability. Every time I stepped outside, even onto the threshold, I feared the man would come barging up to me, prattling insanities and pounding his fists on my body instead of the door.

That fear never went away. I didn't know then just how deeply it would take hold.

CHAPTER 3

I STARE at the paper wall calendar in the kitchen next to the fridge. Beaming Jack-o-lanterns stare back at me with empty, hollow eyes, their mouths stretched wide to reveal a few blocky teeth. I don't know what they have to be so smiley about. They're dead. Someone hacked them open, scooped out their slimy guts, and carved a grin that will last until their bright, shiny skins turn brown and mushy with rot. I see them through the window on these cold October nights, decorating my neighbor's porches, their glow flickering from a distance. People do this every year, selfishly, without any thought to the poor squash, but I won't. It's too gruesome. Too sad. Plus, it draws attention to the house, and I'd rather people look away.

A pen hangs on a string next to the calendar, which I use to cross off today's date, the fifteenth. We're halfway through this ghoulish month. I was enjoying this retro method of date keeping until the first, when, by flipping the harmless September photograph of hay bales and green apple trees, I was reminded of the long stretch of spooky mischief ahead. Neighborhood kids pranking us, smashing eggs on our windows, and leaving bags of dog shit on the porch. The long, dark nights. The urge to curl up by our gas fireplace, easily lighted with the flick of a switch, and lulled to sleep by the heat.

Whooshing from the stove interrupts my thoughts as the water boils. I rip open the blue cardboard box and pour the macaroni elbows into the water, careful not to splash myself.

"Kit?" Mom calls from the other room. "How long?"

"Not much. Gimme ten."

This won't take long to make, which is good 'cause she's hungry. I set the timer and stir the pasta with a wooden spoon. My wrist twinges where I fell on it, not letting me forget, even for a moment, the nightmare in the cemetery.

A yawn catches me by surprise, deep and guttural. I blink and rub my eyes. These late-night episodes are taking their toll. The clock tells me it's past noon. My stomach grumbles despite having a couple of muffins not too long ago. I always nibble on something during my morning schoolwork, but it clearly wasn't enough. I'm hungry too. I need calories fueling my body to stay awake.

I open the meat tray in the fridge, holding my breath against the lingering stink of dead animal flesh, and remove a package of sliced ham. The door closes with a soft thump. I tear the ham into little pieces and set it next to the stove – I'll mix it in with the cheese sauce at the end.

As I prepare the food, my thoughts puzzle over what's happening to me. Whatever it is, it wants me outside. But then what's with the inner compass, that invisible tug that guides me back home? Doesn't that defeat the purpose? It's a weird push-and-pull, like a game. And how does this unexplainable entity make things disappear? My shoes, phone – these items are meant to help me get home safe. Why won't it let me have them? Why make this even more difficult? It's gotta be intentional. An obstacle to keep me from getting home, making me easier prey? How does that even work, anyway? Could it be aliens? For what purpose? To hijack my body for otherworldly science? I can't make heads or tails of it – the whys and hows escape me. What I need is someone to bounce ideas around with, another person who could maybe see things from a different angle. I long to tell Janelle, my best online friend, but would she believe me?

I know I'm lucky to even have a best friend, being the way I am. She lives in the next town over. We met through an internet forum for a game we used to play a couple years ago. We've moved on from that one though. I discovered cozy, real-life simulation while she went on to more violent, horror-themed entertainment. She always liked the thrill while I prefer the steady make-believe of a peaceful world. Even though we veered in different directions, we kept in touch and our friendship grew. She's more outgoing, doesn't suffer the crippling anxiety that holds me back. I find her so inspiring. She can be pretty dark at times, with a certain kind of humor that some people might find disturbing, but to me she's like a breath of fresh air. Although she's tried to get me to come out multiple times, we've never met in person. But that doesn't make our friendship any less valid. Anytime I need to talk, she's there. She always responds and never judges.

But I've never told her anything as strange as this.

Ten minutes later and the macaroni's prepped. I dish it up into a big bowl and push a spoon into the mushy half-moons, burrowing the rounded edge deep into the cheesy depths. A fresh burst of steam curls around the stainless-steel handle, softening the filigree etching and warming my fingers. I inhale the sweet and slightly pungent odor of butter and cheese. The bowl is hot, so I carry it by my fingertips down the hall.

I nudge the open door with my shoulder. The room is dim, but that's normal. Mom's pink velvet curtains are open, but the blinds haven't been lifted in ages. Dust mites swirl in the iridescent glow of the TV. Her familiar mass on the bed stirs as I enter, her fat rolling over every inch of her body as she sits up, from her chin (or rather, lack thereof) to her arms and belly, down to her swollen cankles.

When I say my mother is obese, I'm talking super morbidly – not just as an awful description but as a legitimate classification. Seriously. That's what they call it. I'm not saying this to be mean, it's just a fact. There's no way to say it without sounding like a terrible person.

She's become so large that she can't get up like she used to, can't walk around without the aid of a steel walker, and she gets winded after a few steps. So, she needs lots of help. Her health is failing. She has diabetes. I test her blood sugar a few times a day and give her insulin shots since she can't bear to look at the needle. When she was four hundred pounds she could still get to the bathroom on her own, but that was a long time ago, and now, at more than double that weight, she needs a bed pan. I'm aware the room stinks, I just can't smell it anymore. Every now and then I get a sharp whiff of body odor, the yeasty undertone wafting from her like sourdough. But I'm used to it.

I help feed her every day. When daily tasks got too cumbersome for her, the job of preparing meals gradually shifted to me. I don't mind. It gives me something to do, something to occupy my day. I need all the distractions I can get because my mind is a whirlpool, a deep, swirling hole in my skull where I can get lost. If I get too close, it'll suck me in, and then there's nothing to do but close my eyes and surrender to the force.

You might think I'm a freak for wanting to stay indoors all the time. If you felt what I feel every day, you'd want the same, believe me. Especially now, with the weirdness at night. I wonder if others have this experience...I'd hate to be all alone in this weirdness, but how could I find out? I can't exactly go around asking strangers if they feel the monster in the darkness too. That's a first-class ticket to a padded room, or worse, someone might call Child Protective Services, declare Mom unfit for parenting, and separate us forever. How would she get the care she needs then? I can't risk it; she needs me too much.

"Lunch," I say. Mom's propped up on the bed, her moon face glowing in the light of a daytime talk show. On the screen, heavily made-up women sit around a high table, dangling their expensive stilettos a couple feet off the ground. They look like they should be going to a party rather than talking politics, but there they are. I can't imagine feeling confident enough to speak live on television, so here I am.

I come further into the room and set the bowl on a rolling cart next to the bed. It has a built-in tray that lifts and swivels, bringing the bowl directly under her chin.

"Smells good." She always says this. Grabbing the spoon, she digs around a little before bringing a bite to her mouth. She chews, her lips puckered. The wrinkles of her upper lip, usually hidden beneath the puffiness of her face, briefly appear. After a moment she grunts and sticks a finger between her lips, clearly struggling with something.

"What?" I ask.

She takes forever digging inside her mouth but finally pulls her finger back out and holds something up to the light. I squint – it's hard to see. A curly strand of copper-colored hair.

I shrug. "Maybe it's yours," I tease.

She gives me a look – her hair, though peppered with gray, is mostly the dull brown of stale walnuts. "Kitty, hon. What have I said about tying your hair up when cooking?"

"Okay, fine. Sorry."

She flicks the hair to the floor where it disappears into the dust, lint, and crumbs layering the carpet. Mental note: time to vacuum.

"Did you get that paper done?" she asks.

Schoolwork. Blargh. But I don't complain. I know I'm lucky to be homeschooled, and if I complain, it all might change. "Yes. I did."

"Good girl. You need me to check it?"

I shake my head. She always asks this, as if she participates in my education in any way. My school is online, so it's no big deal. But maybe it's the illusion of helping that counts. Her way of saying "I'm here." The fact that she's willing means a lot, and that's enough for me.

A framed photo of her and Dad on their wedding day sits on her nightstand, and I pick it up. I'm annoyed she keeps it on display like this, but whatever gives her comfort. Rubbing the hem of my shirt across the glass to remove any dust, I ask if she needs anything else.

With her mouth full, she doesn't respond, so I grab the trucker-sized tumbler from her nightstand and shake it. She nods, swallows, and says, "Diet Coke?"

"We're out, but we have lemonade tea. The Splenda one."

"That's fine."

I head back to the kitchen and fill her cup with ice and sweet, lemon-scented tea before moving on to my chores.

Mom can't fit in our standard shower, so she needs traditional sponge baths. She can't bend and reach certain areas to clean, so that's where I come in. I get the lightweight, plastic basin and fill it with warm water. It has a built-in divider, and I add a squirt of pink cherry blossom body wash on one side – the gel makes it foamy and fragrant. I use the clear side to wipe away the soapy residue from her skin. I keep my gaze on the nightstand as I lift her breast and run the cloth underneath the mound, somehow both soft as a feather and heavy as a small sack of flour, making quick work to save us both the embarrassment. It has to be done though. I have to lift her flesh rolls and wipe away the pungent, yeasty jam that accumulates there, especially on her chafed and sweaty lower half. It's delicate work; her skin is always red and raw afterwards.

She says it's humiliating, having me care for her this way, and that she's failing me as a mother. But I don't see it like that. Not at all. Because she needs me, I can always stay here. It's a beautiful situation. Of course, I wish she felt better. I wish she had more energy and didn't need countless medications to get her through the day. Her health took a nosedive as her weight went up. Along with the diabetes came high blood pressure, candida overgrowth, and arthritis. I make sure she gets the right pills at the right times of day. Some need to be taken with food and others on an empty stomach. It's a lot of planning, but I'm doing my best. I prepare all the meals, making sure her portions are well-balanced. The doctor, during her last telehealth visit, sent me downloadable pamphlets, and the internet is full of ideas, but she's always so hungry. She eats more than she should, I know. I just feel bad when she's not satisfied. I'm no chef, but I do my best. I make her vegetables and salads, but you can't live on rabbit food alone. Maybe I'm the one failing her. I can't justify starving my own mother. She gave me life, so I nurture her the way she nurtured me, our roles reversed.

"What's on your mind, Kitty?" she asks.

"Nothing."

She taps my forehead between my eyes. "You're furrowed. What's up?"

I tilt her a little, working on the left side around her waist, talking as I scrub. She winces but I can't be too gentle, no matter how much I wish to spare her discomfort. Better a wince now than festering sores later.

"Janelle's pushing again," I say, talking as I scrub.

"Ah. The movie?"

"Yeah." Scrub, scrub, scrub. I dip the cloth back into the soapy water and swirl it around. "She really wants me to go."

Mom's quiet for a minute as I wipe her down. Then she says, "Well, maybe you should."

I pause, cloth midair. "What?"

"Honey, you've been cooped up in here with me for so long, it might be good for you to get out with friends for a bit. Change of scenery. Get some fresh air."

My face warms. I ignore the fact that the air is now filled with her exposed stench, released from her half-naked body.

"You're young and you should be out there experiencing everything life has to offer. I feel guilty keeping you here all the time. If your dad were still around..."

We tread carefully on this topic. I know she still loves him and her heart broke when he left. She'd take him back if he asked, I imagine, but she's also prone to acting bitter and angry about it. I've never had a romantic partner, obviously, so it goes without saying I've never felt true heartbreak like she has. But when Dad left, he walked out on me too. I can't exactly say that felt good, being left behind like that. My point is, if I'm not careful, she'll go on a rant. I deflect with mirroring – something I read about in my online psych class, where you basically repeat back what someone's saying – and choose my words with care. "If he were still around, he'd probably agree with you."

She nods, her stringy hair falling into her face, covering her eyes. "I just want what's best for you."

"I know."

"It's not healthy, being indoors all the time."

"You're right. I'll try harder."

She looks up at me, sharp. "Try harder? You're not even trying!"

The bite of her tone stings, and I'm taken aback. I stammer a bit, unsure how to respond, and ultimately shut my mouth.

"You sit in your room on your little computer and pretend you're living a real life, but you're not. I'd be remiss if I didn't say anything. I am your mother, after all."

"I-I know that."

"I appreciate all you do around here, but you need to live life outside these walls. At least every once in a while."

I chew the inside of my cheek until it tastes coppery. "We'll see."

I wait for her to say more, but she doesn't press the issue. She seems winded. Mulling over the conversation, we finish her bedside bath in silence. Logically, she has a point. I recognize that. How much would it hurt, really, to make an effort? A flood of all that could go wrong drowns my mind. But the key word here is "could." She's right – I've never tried. Maybe it's time to change that. It's been years since the break-in. Some people say the terrible stuff on the news is fake. I don't dig too deeply in those corners of the internet though, so I don't really know how true that is. Am I ready for this? There's only one way to find out.

Do I have the nerve?

CHAPTER 4

I'M SCRUBBING the macaroni pot when the doorbell rings. I freeze, my arms submerged up to my elbows in hot, lemon-scented bubbles. A quick glance at the clock on the microwave tells me it's not one o'clock yet, so it can't be my groceries. That's supposed to get here between two and three.

Slowly, I pull my arms out of the pot and wipe the suds off with a towel, heart pounding. I can't seem to remember how to blink, my eyes drying out from a wide-eyed stare. If I blink, I could miss a predator looming in my peripheral vision. Every cell in my body trembles from the effort to turn invisible. Oh, how I wish we had a camera trained to the front door, but our income is meager – with Mom on benefits and my issues keeping me from getting a job, we can't afford it. I'd rather budget for deliveries and avoid shopping in-person. Everything we need gets dropped at the door with zero interaction.

My breath comes shallow as I move quietly to the kitchen door and peer down the hall. I wait for the bell to ring again, but it doesn't.

"Kitty?" Mom calls, making me jump. "Aren't you going to get that?"

Geez, could she be *any* louder? "Yes, Mom," I say, my voice hushed. I take another step. Why would the doorbell be ringing so soon? That could be anyone standing outside.

I'm ten again, the man banging on the house and yelling at me with a voice like the devil.

Come on, Kit. You're stronger than this. Get it together. Answer the door. Just open it already.

I slide the deadbolt, keeping the chain in place, just in case. It's not standard for suburban homes to have chain locks, but after Dad left, I installed one myself. It wasn't hard – ten minutes of video instruction and drilling was all it took – and it's worth it for the extra peace of mind. You never know.

Time slows down, each second passing like a drooling drop of honey into tea. I take a deep breath and turn the handle. The door pops open with an ominous squeak. Outside, there is nothing but a brown cardboard box. It's my order after all. An engine rumbles to life and I look up to see the delivery truck moving down the road, on to its next destination. I let out a shaky breath. My hands tremble, and I shake my wrists, rubbing my palms on my jeans to burn off the adrenaline. Everything's fine, no reason to panic. I hoist the heavy box inside and shut the door with my foot.

"Who is it, Kitty?"

"Groceries," I call down the hall. She doesn't respond, but I know she must be a little disappointed. I think on some level she still hopes Dad will come back. I mean, she never took down the photos of him, and his bespectacled face smiles down on me from walls in every room but my own. At sixteen, I'm old enough to let go of such fantasies. I stopped hoping years ago.

I carry the box into the kitchen and rip it open. With a deep sigh, I put everything away: salad mix, eggs, boxes of pasta, cereal, pretzels, and bread. The heavy stuff is at the bottom, cans of veggies and bubble-wrapped jars of marinara. Then I finish cleaning the kitchen. There's more schoolwork to do, but soon I can have a break and watch TV or read or, my favorite, play my online roleplaying game that makes you lose all sense of time and place. Sounds weird but it's super relaxing. When you're indoors all the time you need an escape somehow, and the virtual world can really help with that.

I spray the countertop with some disinfectant and wipe it down with a paper towel. My eyes must be playing tricks on me, though, because in the fragrant streaks a pair of foamy eyes look back at me. I swipe at it with the towel, but two circular orbs remain, outlined by the foamy solution. I scrub at them, hard, and finally the surface is clean. I must be more tired than I thought.

A moth has somehow made its way into my room, its shadow dancing across my sage green walls. I first noticed its gray wings flapping against my vintage travel posters, a dull contrast against the bright, '60s-style images as it took a photographic tour of London, Morocco, and Switzerland. I know it's ironic having these posters, since I can't imagine hopping a plane to any of these places, but the colors are cheery, and I can pretend that I've been to the Eiffel Tower, Big Ben, and the Pyramids. After staring at them on my wall for so long, how impressive would they be, really, in person?

Now the moth plinks against my lamp, nearly falling to the braided, celestial-pattered rug after each *tink*. Then it flies up again, back toward the light, only to fall once more. The noise distracts me, pulling my attention away from my game.

What drives it to do that? I know moths are attracted to light, but dang. It's the equivalent of someone body slamming a wall only to brush themselves off and do it all over again. Why doesn't it move on to another light source? I'm transfixed; I can't take my eyes off the stupid thing.

My phone buzzes with an incoming call. Pulling it closer, I tap the green button and swipe a few strands of hair out of my face. "Hey."

"S'up?" Janelle Martinez's brown face appears washed out in the milky blue glow of her screen, the light occasionally reflecting off her facial piercings in sharp flashes. Starlight constellations adorn her face from her eyebrows down to her chin. I can see her tongue stud when she talks. Sometimes she clicks it against her teeth, which gives me shivers.

"Not much," I say. The moth keeps doing its thing in the background. "Can't sleep. The usual." I don't tell her that I'm avoiding sleep as long as possible, reluctant to experience another night of waking somewhere else.

Tink, tink.

"Yeah, know the feeling."

"So, what's going on?" I ask.

"*Séance of Blood 2.*" She snaps her fingers before pointing at me through the screen. "You. Me. Next weekend. Say you're in."

I groan. This has been a point of tension between us ever since she heard they were filming the horror sequel. Gruesome slasher flicks aren't really my thing, but even if I was in the mood for gallons of fake blood and exaggerated screaming, it goes without saying that I'm gonna watch it at home, not in a theater. And she knows that.

"I know, I know," she says, rolling her eyes. They're so dark brown they look almost black in this lighting, and ringed with thick liquid eyeliner, a beautiful but spooky contrast against her glowing complexion. "But listen. Hear me out. I have that night off from work and I want someone to go with. I want that someone to be you."

"Janelle..."

"Don't 'Janelle' me like my mother. It's time you got out. It'll be fun. You'll face your fears head on and then recover in the dark, cozy cinema, where you can almost pretend you're at home but with a better sound system. It's not like I'm inviting you to a haunted house or something. I mean, I could. 'Tis the season. Would you rather?"

Her devilish grin makes me groan again. "I'm thinking about it, okay? Maybe."

"Bullshit maybe. You *can,* and you *will.*"

"Don't push. Pushing only makes it worse."

She leans back in her chair. "Aww, come on, Kit. Come with me."

"Definitely not opening weekend."

"So...that's a yes?"

"We'll see."

She clicks her tongue stud on her front teeth, sending tiny electric zips through my nervous system. "What if I ask nicely? Please?"

I allow myself to imagine what it would be like to meet Janelle in person, to feel a friendly hug, the warmth of human contact. I don't get that from Mom, not really. Because of her size, she's not comfortable being touched anymore. She complains her skin stretches so tightly these days it aches. But I also know she's embarrassed, sometimes she cries about it when she thinks I can't hear. I feel so helpless when that happens. I try so hard to help her, to take care of us both, but sometimes I think it's impossible. Some days I want to break down too. I'm sure it will take just one small thing to make me crack. That's why I struggle with going to the movies with Janelle. It's too much. I want to hate her for asking, but she's just trying to help. The comparison is not lost on me.

I shrug.

"Hey, listen," Janelle says, voice smoothing out like caramel. I imagine it's the tone one uses with a wild animal to keep it calm. "Don't be mad, but have you ever considered, like, maybe talking to someone about this?"

"Like, therapy?" Honestly, I've thought about it. But opening up to a complete stranger feels impossible, and what if they judged me or Mom and how we live? It might not be ideal, but it's comfortable. It works. In the back of my mind, however, thoughts of turning eighteen, becoming an adult, and the expectations that brings creep up to the surface. I tamp it down. That's ages from now. There's time to figure that out. And if, at that point, I need to talk to someone about it, then I'll reconsider.

For now, I shake my head.

"It might help," Janelle says.

"I don't know. Can we talk about this later?"

She chuckles. "One of these days I'm getting you out into the real world. It's not so bad. You should try it sometime."

I recall the cemetery last night and shudder.

A wooden bang followed by a cacophony of voices fills my speaker as Janelle rolls her eyes. "One sec," she says, before spinning her chair to confront the source of the noise. Over her shoulder, I glimpse one male torso in a red basketball jersey, and a separate arm covered by what appears to be a cable-knit sweater. Bits of human in my screen, fragmented bodies like leftover puzzle pieces. I assume they are her brothers. I know she has a few.

"Get the fuck out of here," Janelle growls in a voice I've never heard her use before. "What are you even doing?"

"Yo," a deep voice, rumbly like an earthquake, meets my ears. "You gotta move your car."

"It's late."

"Nah, you don't understand. Kiana's invited me over. You know? And you're blocking me in."

The second voice pipes up, higher and creakier than the first. "He can't. You can't. She's Nathan's ex, and you know full well they're gonna get back together, and then you'll be toast. It's better if you stay. Don't move your car, Jan."

"I am a grown-ass man and I will see whoever the fuck I want to. It's *Kiana*."

"You're a *dead man*. I'm trying to save you, dude."

Janelle cracks her neck, her long, blue-black hair swishing dramatically from side to side with each loud pop. "Children," she says, clearly annoyed. "You've interrupted a very important phone call for some actual bullshit. Whatever." She spins back around to face me and scrunches her nose. "Sorry, I'll be right back, 'kay? Just think about it while I'm gone. Don't hang up."

Janelle's black leather chair spins in her wake. I chew on my cuticles, waiting for her return, inspecting the nailbeds I've demolished in an obsessive, trancelike state. The squeak of Janelle's chair brings my attention back to the screen. Only it's not Janelle who greets me. This guy's the spitting image of Janelle, only more masculine. Same dark hair, brown eyes, tan skin. Her brother, maybe?

"Hi," he says.

"Oh." I drop my hand into my lap, hangnails raw and stinging. "Um. Hey."

"So, you're Kit."

My eyes dart left and right as I scramble for words. I can't think of a response.

"I hear you've got some problems."

I stiffen. "What?"

He smiles, holding his hands up. "It's okay, I'm not here to judge."

So why is he here?

"What are you talking about? What's Janelle told you about me?"

"I know you're agoraphobic. That you never leave your house. That you struggle with anxiety and even a bit of depression. That you won't seek help for it."

A strange, creeping warmth fills my body as I'm washed in equal parts mortification and rage toward Janelle for spilling my business.

"That's why I'm here. I can be your friend; you just have to trust me."

"How can I – why would I trust you? I don't even know you." My foot jiggles with nervous energy.

"Then get to know me." His dark eyes pierce mine, and I stab the red button, ending the call without warning. I turn my phone screen down as if I can hide the strange interaction. What was that all about?

My phone rings again, and it's Janelle. If I answer, will that guy be the one that greets me, angry now that I've hung up on him? But Janelle said she'd be right back, so I take a chance and answer.

Relief floods my body as her image fills my screen. "Sorry about that," she says. "They're fucking annoying."

My relief burns hot as it shifts into anger. "Why'd you tell your brother about my issues?"

"Huh?"

"One of your brothers sat down when you left and started saying all this stuff about me. Stuff he'd only know if you'd told him. So why are you talking about me?"

Her eyes widen and her mouth drops open. "I didn't – I haven't! I swear. Who was it?"

"I don't know, he didn't give me his name. He looked, well, he looked like you."

"Genes are strong in our family; we all share similarities." She shakes her head. "Maybe he overheard our conversation? But I haven't said anything, promise. Your business is yours alone. Well, and mine. I really wanna hang out with you."

My anger dissipates, the emotional whiplash taking a toll as my shoulders drop and my voice softens.

"I know. I'm working on it. Really."

We spend the next hour keeping each other company as we play our respective games. When we hang up, the room seems eerily quiet. I'm reminded of how isolated I've become. It's always a sharp contrast, that feeling I get after being social, busy, and happy online. I stare at my game's pause screen on my laptop. The urge to play has lessened as fatigue seeps into my bloodstream, overpowering the caffeine I'd consumed earlier. When I shut down the computer, the silence in the room presses down on me further, like solid weight. It's not unpleasant, just noticeable.

A thick yawn fills my throat, warning that sleep is imminent. Which reminds me of a more pressing matter. I can't wake up outside again – who knows what will happen the next time I do. Locking the door didn't stop me. Even my sleepwalking self seems to understand how locks work. So, I must stop myself from moving around.

I dig out a cardboard box in my closet labeled "Winter Things." It smells of must and coats my fingers with a layer of gray dust when I open it. Rooting around the mittens, hats, and extra fuzzy socks, I find what I'm looking for – a long scarf in a garish pink and yellow polka dot print that hurts my eyes. I haven't worn it since I was a kid.

Taking it to the bed, I bend over and wrap it around both of my ankles, tying the flannel material as tight as I can until my legs resemble a mermaid tail. I'm hoping that if I get up in the night, I'll trip and awaken before even reaching my door. It feels dumb, but I've got to try. Anything to keep me here.

CHAPTER 5

THE FIRST TIME I woke up outside was a couple of weeks ago, on the first of the month. My dreams, the only ones I can remember now, were filled with starbursts. My eyes were neither open nor closed, but within them a glittery spectacle of silent fireworks stole my attention. Mesmerized by the images, drawn toward the show, I drifted forward as if weightless, my toes pointing behind me. I couldn't see the ground with my eyes filled with light, but it had to be there, as I floated higher and higher, like a helium balloon. If I touched the lights they'd feel like golden velvet, soft and comforting. I had to reach them.

But as I got closer to the explosions, I woke up.

Heart palpitations rattled me awake, and I could tell immediately that I wasn't in bed.

I was lying on something hard and lumpy. The ground. I felt it beneath my palms, firm and crumbly. Dirt. Oh my God. I was outside. I opened my eyes. A sound rustled not far to my left. I froze, motionless, my breath shallow. What was that? An animal? There weren't many trees, so it couldn't be branches blowing and scraping in the wind.

I shivered, exposed without a coat and vulnerable to the elements. How did I get there? Did I sleepwalk? But where? I didn't recognize my surroundings. It was dark, nighttime still, but I didn't have a watch... or my phone. I reached in my pocket, unsure of what was happening. Where did it go? It was too weird. It had to be a dream. A very bad dream. Well, okay, let's call it what is really was: a freaking nightmare.

Bushes, pale and stiff with frost framed my left side. To my right, a small mound of earth marred an otherwise perfectly manicured lawn. A smooth, white stone placed on top had words etched into it. Squinting, I leaned closer to read what it said. "Here lies Scruffy, loved and missed." Someone's pet was buried in this backyard.

I had to get out of there before someone saw me. Turned out this backyard belonged to a house on my street, only a few mailboxes down from my own. I ran, my bare feet slapping against the cold, rough sidewalk.

My front door was locked. So was the sliding back door to the kitchen. Walking to the front, I pondered the situation. I must've sleepwalked. But I didn't have a house key on me, so I couldn't have locked it on my way out. Mom must have gotten up and done it, thinking I was safe in bed. But she's never done that before, it's too difficult for her. I'm the one that closes the house at night. I swallowed these unsettling thoughts.

I dropped to my knees and moved the frog, hoping the neighbors wouldn't see as I dug at the ground, clumps of cold, hard soil lodging beneath my fingernails. I grasped the metal key.

Home never felt so good.

That first week, every other night I'd find myself awake a little bit further from the house, in various neighbors' yards, until recently when the disappearances – or whatever you call it – ramped up to a whole new level.

Now, every night I find myself in places I've never been before, places I've never seen, every time I go under. Mostly parks and playgrounds, but now the cemetery. I haven't told Mom. I don't want her to worry, I do enough of that for the both of us. I wonder if the subconscious part of my brain is aching for a change of scenery and that's why this is happening – some deeper part of me is propelling my body out of the house when my defenses are down. That's possible, right?

Except my feet, always bare, are clean.

However I'm getting to these places, I'm not sleepwalking. The thought makes me shiver. I've tried everything to stop it. Locking the doors and windows doesn't work. Keeping my phone in my pocket doesn't ensure it stays with me. I once set up my phone to record the front door, but in the morning when I checked, it was blank, as if I'd forgotten to start it. I'm hoarding energy drinks in my room like the apocalypse is near and use eye drops during the day to hide the redness from Mom. I figure if I don't sleep, I won't disappear.

If only it were that simple.

———

I'm draped across a stack of shrink-wrapped hay bales. Not real ones, I discover, but smaller, cheaply bound packages meant only for decoration, according to the stickers plastered over them. I push myself upright, toppling some of the hay in the process. The scarf is gone, probably lying in a heap on my bedroom floor. I probably untied it in my sleep – I am my own worst enemy. My skin tightens with the feeling of being watched. The sensation is getting familiar, but it's no less disconcerting. Slowly, I look over my shoulder and wince. An evil clown stretching as tall as the ceiling looms over me, wearing a straw hat and a sadistic, blood-red grin that splits its face in half. It wields a pitchfork dipped in blood. A price tag dangles from its weapon, stating it can be purchased for $189.99 as part of a haunted farm collection.

This is a Halloween store, the kind that only opens for a month or two and provides horrific goods for connoisseurs of the spooky season.

I kick a hay bale out of my way and clock the glowing red EXIT sign at the opposite end of the building.

I make my way carefully in that direction, passing a wall lined with a collection of masks in a variety of shapes, colors, and gore. Their relentless dead eyes stare at me, watching as I move through the store. I pass through shoulder-height aisles offering rubberized limbs coated with fake blood, bags of polyester spiderwebs, and zombie figurines. In the dim, red security lighting, everything looks extra sinister. The air smells like vinyl and sweet cherry candy.

A cacophony sends my heart skittering in my chest. A screaming, ten-foot-tall grim reaper invades my personal space, rocking gleefully back into neutrality. His scythe mechanically clicks back by his side, quiet now that its purpose has been fulfilled. I hurry away from it before it goes off again, but motion sensors detect my body, and a little Victorian girl sings a creepy lullaby while a trademarked serial killer plays his theme song before taking a swipe at me with his famous machete. Shouldn't these things be turned off at night?

Finally reaching the checkout counter, I approach the glass double doors that lead outside. They're blacked out with images of smiling children in costumes, oblivious to the horrors of the world. I undo the latches, thankful I don't need a key to unlock the store from the inside.

An alarm blares with a high-pitched beeping that follows me into the night.

CHAPTER 6

JANELLE INSISTS I go with her to the movies. It doesn't matter how much I protest, she keeps asking. Or rather, telling, in her own bossy way. I guess that's what happens when you have brothers. I don't have a problem standing up to her, it's just when I explain my hesitation, she won't listen.

"Come on," she says. "What have you got to lose by going?"

"Um, my sanity?"

She scoffs. "Right. You're just psyching yourself out. How do you know you won't like it if you never even try?"

"Hey, that's not fair. I do try."

"When?" She looks pointedly at me through the screen. "By getting the mail? Stepping a whole six feet outside your house?"

"It's more than six feet," I mumble under my breath. It's more like fifteen. I know, because I counted. Her words sting, but I try not to let it show. "I gotta go. It's time for Mom's bath."

"This isn't the end, you know."

But it is. It has to be. Who knows how much worse things can get out there.

———

My self-imposed isolation was gradual. Though I completely freaked out about the aggressive drunk, I still had to go to school and piano lessons and run errands with Mom. But it was that defining moment that lifted the veil of innocence and showed me that some things in life are a little off kilter and potentially dangerous. That's a pretty tough lesson for a ten-year-old. I started watching the news, a few minutes here and there, to see if the man would show up on screen, having bothered someone else. And that's when I learned there are far worse things than being yelled at.

There's not a lot you can say to convince me that the world is safe. A lot can go wrong. The daily news taught me that. There's always a shooting, a new disease, or threat of nuclear war – apocalyptic stuff. My worldview changed with each headline, blurred photo, and ominous tone the anchors adopted. I know innocence doesn't last forever, but no kid ever expects to lose it. And why would they? From birth, we're shielded in the loving cocoon of our parent's embrace, fed, nurtured, and safe. Nothing to fear. But then we grow up. We learn to walk, and we walk away from the bubble wrap of our parent's love. Why would we *want* to do that?

Now, I know better.

They waited almost a year before leaving me on my own again. They'd been invited to an adults-only dinner party, the kind where Dad's boss would be in attendance. I sat crisscross applesauce on my bed as he explained this, dressed in his nicest suit and tie, while I picked the fraying hem of my yellow baby blanket, unspooling threads from an embroidered duckling in the corner. "I can't not go, honey," he said.

I let my face show my displeasure. "Why not?"

"Sometimes grown-ups have to socialize. It's called 'networking,' and someday you'll understand."

"Why can't Mom stay with me, then? She doesn't go to your work."

"Because we already RSVP'd as a couple. They're expecting

her. It would be rude if she didn't turn up. You get it." He ruffled my hair, but I couldn't let it go.

"How come you don't get a babysitter?"

"They're all busy tonight, kiddo, and you're old enough to try spending a couple of hours alone. The length of a movie."

"Which movie?"

"Katherine." He sighed. "It'll be okay. You're ready. We won't be far if you need us."

My heart leaped into my throat. I didn't feel ready. I didn't think I'd ever be ready again. I followed Dad out of my room, insisting on a babysitter. "Laura's pretty fun, she plays games with me."

"Laura has prom tonight, sweetie." Mom fussed with her hair in the mirror, the same mirror I now associate with my own terrified reflection. I avoided looking into it for months, averting my eyes when walking by. "She can't do it. Most of our regular sitters are going to prom. Besides, your father's right. You can stay here for a bit. It's just dinner. We won't be late. We trust you not to burn the house down." She chuckled, but I didn't find her joke very funny. It wasn't me I was worried about. It was other people. The ones outside.

Despite my begging, they went off into the night, waving and blowing kisses as they left. The house was quiet, and I didn't dare turn on any music like before. I sat on the couch in the living room, listening to the house as it settled. I watched the clock, counting the seconds until Mom and Dad came home. It was rhythmic, soothing, a chant in my head (one hundred and thirty-seven, thirty-eight, thirty-nine...) I got lost in the cadence. I was up to four hundred before a strange creak broke my concentration.

It wasn't the usual kind of crack and pop the house made every night, the sound of wood acclimating to the chill of sundown. No, this was slow, more distinct. Deliberate. It came from the kitchen. I stared in that direction, unblinking, waiting. It happened again, not really a creak but more of a groan. Not like wood when it strains beneath weight, but like a human in pain.

I swallowed a lump in my throat as my heart jackhammered inside my chest. The groan moved closer to the kitchen door. Louder. Closer to me. Part of me wanted to get up and investigate. Mostly I wanted to sink into the cushions and become invisible, in case the boogeyman had finally come to get me.

The kitchen door opened. A figure lurched through the doorway and paused, grabbing the frame for balance.

It wasn't the boogeyman.

It was a real man.

Whether it was the same guy that had banged on our door the year before or someone new, I'll never know. All I know is that he was older, grisly, with wrinkles all over his face and unkempt clothing that reeked of fried food and B.O. His teeth were coated in brown sludge.

He must've come in through the back door. So preoccupied with the front of the house, I didn't check to see if the back was locked. Rookie mistake, even for a kid. It was probably all too easy for him to get inside.

His wild eyes frantically darted around the living room.

I should've run, but I couldn't. My brain couldn't process what I was seeing – my ultimate fear, a stranger breaking into the house, coming true. Did I make it happen by thinking about it too much? Was this my fault? The man coughed, a wet hacking sound that nearly convinced me he'd pass out from lack of oxygen. But he didn't. Whatever byproduct ended up in his mouth, he swallowed it with a grimace before settling his gaze on me. My stomach swooped, knowing this wasn't good, but my brain and legs would not cooperate. They couldn't. My phone was on the end table, but if I reached for it, would he get there faster? And then what?

He gripped the front of his pants, moaning as the fabric darkened and a new stench filled the room – he'd peed himself. I closed my eyes to make myself invisible. But I didn't like not knowing where he was in the room, so I opened them again.

We locked eyes for what seemed like hours. Time slowed and

lost all meaning. It was like we were connected in a strange, cosmic way, but I still couldn't figure out what he wanted. Was he a thief? Was I being kidnapped? Or was he just lost and needed a bathroom?

I held my breath and leaned, slowly, reaching for my phone. He cried out, a horrible, gurgling sound, and moved toward me with an unexpected quickness, becoming a blur that shoved me to the ground. My ankle twisted beneath me, sparkling fireworks of pain. And then he was gone, my phone with him, the front door swinging into the wall with a bang.

My parents found me later that night, shaken with fear and full of hot rage that they had left me. They called the police, but it was a lost cause. The damage had already been done. If panic and pain can bleed into the places where you're meant to be safe, it must be even worse beyond these four walls. That's when I decided I would never set foot outside again.

CHAPTER 7

I'M in bed later that night, thinking about what Mom said. I realize, despite my objection, that she has a point. It isn't good to be indoors twenty-four-seven like this. I get zero exercise except for the yoga stretches I do a couple times a week, no sunlight, and I'm constantly getting sick, probably from the stale air in the house that allows bacteria and germs to breed and multiply at a horrifying rate. I was so active as a kid, dancing ballet and running around the park. Yoga is the closest thing I have to my old life, The Before. Maybe it's not enough. Maybe I should take Janelle up on her offer, you know, for health.

But, God, the thought alone sets my heart racing. I press my hand to my chest and feel the rapid thumping beneath my sternum. There's no way I can do it. I'd probably collapse. I know it doesn't make sense to only feel safe in the one place where everything bad has happened, but it doesn't make it any less true. How can I leave? But then again, maybe waking up outside is my psyche telling me I'm ready. What if the creature is merely a figment of my imagination, a subconscious ploy to get some cardio? Maybe Mom's right: how do I know unless I try – really try?

Before the world broke me, ballet was my life. I started classes at three, twirling around with glee with my fellow ballerinas, and it brought so much happiness to my life. The satin bodice of my recital tutu was cool and smooth beneath my fingers, and all during my first performance, I rubbed my tummy in awe. The scratchy skirt flared out as I leaped and plied and shimmied. Each year I got better.

Then it all came to a stop. After that first night alone, I refused to go. I'd caught a glimpse of some ugliness in the world; how could the beauty of dance exist in the same space as fear and uncertainty?

No more twirls for me.

I do miss the tactile sensation of the tutu, however. Touch is such a great stress relief. The action of rubbing something silky between my fingers triggers a calming in my brain and my body relaxes. That's why I have a satin pillowcase. Mom ordered it for Christmas for me, and it's probably my favorite thing in my bedroom. It's a gorgeous shade of emerald and the material feels perpetually cool and slippery against my skin. Bonus, it keeps my curls from frizzing too badly at night. When I lay down and rub my cheek on it, I feel something almost akin to joy. It takes me back to those ballerina days of my youth, of innocence, of doing something just because you love it.

Now, I practice yoga in my living room. I follow along with videos a couple times a week as a form of exercise and meditation. It helps to calm and soothe my rattled nerves, or at least I like to think it does. At the very least, I'm getting some movement during the day.

Not that I'm deluded into thinking it's anything too strenuous. I'm certainly not flexible enough to call myself a yogi. But for thirty minutes twice a week, usually after school but before dinner, I move the coffee table and unroll my pink yoga mat in front of the TV. It feels good to stretch and center myself. It's the one thing my body thanks me for these days. Because sitting at a desk, or on the bed, or the couch, day in and day out does a number on my back. It's constantly sore; I'm always rubbing it like an old person. I feel ancient.

I think about this as my back twinges while I fold clothes in our tiny, cramped laundry room. It's no more than a closet, really. Perhaps it was, in a past life, and someone gutted the shelves to make room for a stacked washer and dryer. If I close the door behind me while facing the machines, my backside presses up against it. I suppose it's a good use of space though. The idea of a massive laundry room doesn't make much sense to me. Usually, I'll dump the hot clothes in a basket and carry it to the living room and watch TV, but today I'm lost in thought. It's a mindless task, a meditative chore. The fabric rustles between my fingers as I fold shirts and sweatpants. Each flap of the material releases a burst of fragrant detergent that clogs my nose with an artificially sweet scent.

I stop folding. How many times have I done this? Too many to count. We change linens quite frequently. Mom sweats like you wouldn't believe. Her pillowcases need changing almost every morning. What is the average amount of folding done by a sixteen-year-old? Have I done this too much for someone my age? Does Janelle even do laundry? I shake my head and resume my task. No, no, it's fine. I want this. It's better this way. Small thing to exchange for the serenity of being at home.

The single lightbulb above my head flickers as if in response to my thoughts. I look up and watch as it dims and brightens, as if it can't decide whether to stay on. The bulb must be on its last leg and needs replacing soon. I better add it to my online shopping basket. Sigh. There's always something.

Something plops onto my head. It felt like a raindrop. Looking up, there's nothing on the ceiling to indicate a leak, no dark spots, no moisture. So, what was it? I shake my hair, dislodging whatever it is, and it hits the floor with hardly a sound.

I crouch to inspect the small, white thing. It's round and

ridged, no bigger than the tip of my finger. It unfurls itself and wriggles sort of like a drunken inchworm across the floor. Is that... a maggot? My hands react instinctively, raking my hair to remove any of its creepy, crawly friends. But he's the only one. How did it get there? Maggots don't live in ceilings, right? I think of termites, ants, and roaches – insects you might expect to infiltrate a home. But maggots bring to mind flesh, rotten from death. Without thinking, I stomp on the repulsive creature, squishing it beneath my slipper. Regret drenches me, and not just because I need to scrape the goo off my sole. No, something like guilt pricks at my innards, like I've just done something horrific. But it's a bug – it's not real murder, right? But something doesn't feel right. I keep expecting another one to fall.

Eyes flicking constantly to the ceiling, I resume folding the laundry.

The light stays on for the duration of my task.

CHAPTER 8

IT'S three fourteen in the morning and I've yet to fall asleep. If I can stay awake until dawn, the safety of sunlight might protect me from the so-called sleepwalking mystery – I hope. Sighing, I get up to use the bathroom, stopping for a long drink of water from the steel bottle on my nightstand. Waiting out the night is thirsty work. The caffeine does a number on my bladder, putting it in overdrive. Which, of course, makes me thirstier. It's a vicious cycle.

I pad barefoot into the hall, quietly, so I don't wake Mom, and move on soft feet to the bathroom. Flicking on the light, I squint and rub the corners of my eyes before peeling down my bottoms and settling on the toilet seat. At first, I don't notice anything different. But as I relieve myself, it slowly dawns on me that it sounds... different. Not like the usual water hitting water. It's more like water hitting a bowl full of rubber balls or something. A muted sound.

The light above the sink dims and flares, just like the bulb in the laundry room. What are the odds these lights need changing too?

I finish, stand up to flush – and revulsion sends a wave of bile up my throat. I cover my mouth to keep from vomiting, which would add to the disgusting sight. The toilet bowl is full of wriggly, squirmy maggots, like the one in the laundry room. How did they get there? Fuck! I squeeze my eyes shut and wish it all away. I've fallen asleep and this is my new nightmare, I just know it. I open my eyes and, to my utter disappointment, find that the horrible larvae still writhe inside the porcelain bowl. If I flush, will it clog? Or will they simply wash away down the pipe?

I want to call out for Mom. I want her to take care of this, like the parent she's supposed to be.

There it is, the rare, dark thought I never explore, the one I keep pushed down inside and cover up with ideas of independence and competence. Most of the time it doesn't bother me. But this? This is gross. Why is it put on me? That's so unfair. I'm weak. I'm human. I'm only sixteen – I'm allowed to feel this way. But whining about it won't solve the problem, and what can Mom do that I can't?

I suck it up, grit my teeth and, after making sure the plunger's handy, flush and wait for the upsurge of larvae.

After the bathroom fiasco, I email a local exterminator, asking for a quote. I'm prepared to suck it up and handle a stranger in the house if it means getting rid of the disgusting pests. I press "send" and stare at my laptop, about to pop some caffeine tablets, when I consider setting up a camera again. I've tried recording the front door to no avail, as the video stops when I walk back to the hallway, and I'm left with nothing. But now I'll try recording myself sleeping and get to the bottom of this.

Angling the screen so the camera captures my bed feels super weird and icky, like I'm preparing for a dirty video or something. But it's only for me, and I'll be fully dressed, and it could put my mind at ease. That's worth any initial discomfort in setting up. If I can see how it happens, maybe I can stop it. I've tried locking my door and window, but maybe I unlock them in my sleepwalking state.

For once I'm looking forward to bedtime. I'm finally getting some answers. What if I'm too excited to fall asleep?

I prepare warm milk with honey and slather up with Mom's lavender scented hand cream, hoping the aromatherapy will help me relax. I touch record on my camera and then climb under the covers.

In that space again, surrounded by velvet stars, I forget what I was worried about. A sweet scent fills my nose, earthy and somehow sugary, like carob chips we once tried in a cookie recipe in place of actual chocolate. I bask in this feeling of relaxation and relief from tension. My head, despite turning into pudding-like mush, says this is wrong, but my heart disagrees. Which one is right? I let my body take over, the craving for whatever lurks in this blissful space urging me forward, sideways, seeking the source of it, but never finding.

My palms slip on gravel as I push myself to a sitting position.

As usual, I'm somewhere else.

A long alleyway, with two brick walls looming on either side, pressing in as though to squeeze me out. But it's just my imagination. They aren't moving – it's just a tight, narrow space.

I'm not alone. There are people here – crouching, leaning against the wall, laying on the ground as if asleep, just like I was a moment ago. A body curled up beneath a worn-out blanket has skin so pale it's almost blue, but they're not shivering or anything to show they're cold.

Oh, dear God, please let that person be sleeping.

Broken glass and needles litter the path before me. I pick around them on my tiptoes the best I can, trying not to draw attention to myself, but it doesn't matter. It seems no one cares that I'm here. A sliver of glass embeds itself in my big toe, and I hiss. Fighting tears, I start running, but the glass in my foot forces me to slow down which goes against every instinct. Leaning against the gritty brick wall, I lift my foot and examine the wound. It's too dark to really see it, and too small to remove without tweezers anyway. My shoulders hunch and curl to get my body into the fetal position, my usual response to pain and fear. I'd love to give in, but not with strangers around, and not on this filthy ground. I'll just have to endure it – what's a little pain compared to what's coming for me anyway?

The thought alone sets my heart racing.

I keep moving. My head down, gaze on the ground, until a cough barks out from the right. I lock eyes with a scrawny man. His clothes are tattered and his hair limp and greasy. His face is pockmarked with scars, maybe from acne or a fire burn, or scratching with his fingernails. His eyes, a startling clear blue, follow me as I pick my way through the alley. He reminds me of the intruder when I was a kid, and goosebumps ripple down my arms. He watches me as I walk, unblinking. I expect him to lunge or something, though it's clear I have nothing valuable to take.

Unless it's something else he has on his mind.

The bumps migrate from my arms to my neck. I'm vulnerable out here, with not even a coat to protect my skin. My ears, hyper-sensitive to every sound, pick up on the crunch of footsteps behind me. I walk faster, no longer feeling the pain in my feet, the scrapes, the cuts, the bruises going completely unnoticed. The footsteps quicken to match my pace.

And then a shift in the air, that feeling of something coming out of the shadows.

I bolt, freaked, no longer caring what I step on in my haste to get out of here. I run so fast; all I can hear is the sound of my breathing. My breath drowns out everything around me, huffing and puffing filling my ears, blood pumping through my veins with a bass-like thrum. It doesn't matter, nothing here matters – the only place that matters is home. I must get home.

———

I got it. I can't believe this.

After the usual, unexplainable navigation home, I immediately check the footage on my computer.

There I am, in bed, dozing off. I speed up the video until something drastic makes me stop and rewind, then play it at normal speed.

My body stills with what must be sleep, no longer tossing and turning. The very next second – I'm gone. Poof. Not there.

My mouth drops while I fast forward through the minutes until I storm back in and my haunted face fills the screen before it abruptly ends. I replay the footage over and over again. I watch it hundreds of times, just to be sure. And every time, like a magic trick, I blink out into nothingness, my rumpled blankets collapsing into the space where my body was.

How much time passed between my disappearance and return? I check the timestamp. It's all played out in real time, strangely enough. But this is major. Actual proof of something... unexplainable.

I'm not crazy.

I look over my shoulder as the creepiness of it all comes over me. I hug myself and stare at the video where I paused it – seconds before I disappear. What on earth is it? Something paranormal? I hate using that word, it always seemed made up by people too lazy to figure out the science of something. Is it something to do with matter – atoms and glitches in the space-time continuum? Is that even a thing? My initial excitement fades the more I puzzle over it, trying to connect the dots. All I know is that I'm left with more questions than answers, and that doesn't make me feel any better.

In the morning, I receive a reply from the exterminator saying that maggots aren't something they can help with but encourage me with some tips to get rid of them on my own. I bleach and toss all our meat (even the fresh stuff that's still very much in date, just in case). I scrub the garbage bins and liberally spray insecticide to no avail. Maggots continue showing up all over the house, in places least expected. I pour vinegar and salt and lime on them. Nothing works. We don't live in filth, per se. Our house is pretty average when it comes to cleanliness. I do my best. But I can't live like this, with bugs crawling around, crawling *toward* me, and it feels as if the maggots are doing it on purpose. They don't bother Mom. She's never seen them. I hate the way her eyebrows scrunch when I ask, as if I'm a puzzle she can't figure out. It's like they're targeting me alone, trying to push me out of the house by making it unbearable. And the internet isn't helping my mindset, with all the images of the horrible things crawling out of people's faces and stuff like that. Gross. On the bright side, it's harder falling asleep knowing they'll show up anywhere, any time. I'm paranoid they'll crawl into my ears, up my nose, or inside my mouth if I relax. I'm a nervous wreck. Well, more so than usual.

Bags appear beneath my eyes, dark, bruised, and puffy. I can't focus on my schoolwork, and my last assignment received the lowest grade I've ever had. I play my games on autopilot, not really feeling it. I pound caffeine like an addict, my tolerance building, needing more and more for the same mild effect each day. I ignore the bitter taste of coffee and chug it like medicine.

I'm preparing dinner. I've made a meatloaf since it's Mom's favorite, but with a lighter, vegetarian twist – plant-based protein instead of beef, to cut the saturated fat. Mom said she'd try it; she really is making an effort now. I've prepared the loaf and open the oven door to slide it in, but before I can pull back, the door slams on my arm.

"Ahh!"

The heat comes through the fabric of my sleeve, pressing against my skin like a flat iron. I yank the door back open and pull my singed arm free. "What? How?" I whine to myself as I cradle my arm to my chest. Thank God I'm wearing long sleeves – if I wasn't, who knows what would've happened. I inspect my arm and see the black, charcoal-like soot from the dirty oven door smeared on my sleeve. But why did it close? In all my time cooking, that's never happened, not once. What made it slam so hard? Faulty hinge? I open the door with a firm grip on the handle, just in case, and experiment with opening and closing it. It squeaks a little in protest, but it's not springy or anything.

I look at the meatloaf in dismay. It overturned on the rack when I dropped it in surprise, and the contents have spilled through to the bottom where they're already getting crusty and brown. Great.

Donning rubber gloves as well as cushiony oven mitts for extra protection, I wipe out the mess to the best of my ability.

I dig out the can of oven cleaner buried in the collection of soaps, sprays, and detergents under the sink. I spray generously and watch as the foam on the door bubbles and spreads to create an image. A face. I'm reminded of the eyes I imagined not too long ago on the counter. This is different. Not only are there are a pair of eyes appearing as two dark pockets in the sinking froth, but a nose, mouth, and chin. I'm meant to wait before scrubbing, to let the chemicals do their work, but I take my sponge and wipe it anyway. The face should've smeared. It doesn't. What gives? I examine the label of the can to see if there's any explanation, but there isn't one. I rub it again, concentrating hard on it, but it doesn't go away. The foam doesn't dissolve, and those eyes burn into my soul. Unease settles deep in my belly, like grease.

Is it a ghost? Is my house haunted?

Am *I*?

I squeeze out the sponge and spray more foam on top of the face. I scour it with every ounce of muscle until the oven door is finally clear. That was weird.

When the oven is sparkling again, I rip off the gloves with a snap. My shoulders slouch from exhaustion. Not only did I have a mess to clean up, but now there's another meal to prepare from scratch. What if it happens again? I can't deal with appliances that bite and suds that scowl.

Sandwiches are fine for now. But what will happen tomorrow?

CHAPTER 9

ICE COLD PRESSURE pushes down on my body, my limbs akimbo, drifting at odd angles. I gasp, shocked, but swallow a mouthful of chlorinated water, choking with a burbling sound as it burns my esophagus and fills my lungs. Alarmed, I open my eyes, and they sting in darkness. My blurry vision adjusts to what little light there is up above me, a pale blue glow.

A pool. It must be. I'm in the deep end, the surface rippling overhead and taunting me with release.

I can't swim. I never learned. When most kids were having swim lessons, I was doing ballet, and then nothing at all. I have a vague memory of a picnic by the river, splashing in shallow water as Mom and Dad watched protectively, shouting warnings about staying close to shore. There may have been discussion of signing me up for lessons, but obviously that never happened.

The surface isn't too far above my head, ten feet, maybe, less distance than my mailbox, but I don't know how to reach it. I kick my legs in slow motion, the heaviness of the water fighting against me. My body sinks lower, scraping and skimming the rough concrete of the pool floor. Gliding along the bottom, I feel around with my hands. My lungs ache for oxygen – how long have I been under?

There must be a ladder, somewhere, but it's too dim and my vision is too distorted to tell. If I can pull myself up...

I've got to find a wall. That's my only way out. The lack of air brings starbursts to my eyes and a flailing sense of panic to my extremities as I scoop my arms through the water, frustratingly, terrifyingly slow. My body feels simultaneously weightless and bogged down, a clash of sensation, as I drag myself across the bottom, zaps of desperation electrifying my lungs, my head, and my brain, each fighting for the last molecules of stale breath inside me that I fear have already been spent. Squinting to make sense of shapes in the wavering darkness, I find a set of horizontal rungs – a ladder. It doesn't reach the bottom, though; it doesn't even come halfway. I can't reach it from where I stand. Still, I make my way in that direction. The wall is the same rough material as the floor, and I spread my hands wide and press as I jump, leveraging the grittiness beneath my grip to sort of push and pull myself up.

It doesn't work. The water keeps it slippery, and my hands slide down as I sink again. No time to think about it – I try again, jumping a little, kicking my feet. Nope.

Again. I jump, bending my knees into a crouch, and touch the wall with my toes. I reach up, using momentum to push off with my feet, keeping my hands on the wall. I didn't sink as far that time.

Again. Dynamite explodes in my chest as my brain goes fuzzy. I lose all thought. This is animalistic, a survival instinct. I'll have no other chance. My energy wanes, and it's all I can do to maintain this inch-worming motion to the top. My life is whittled down to scaling this wall. If I don't ascend...

I don't wonder if I'll make it. I don't think about what'll happen if I don't. I don't think about how glorious that breath of air will be –

I break the surface, gripping the rounded lip of the pool, and haul myself over the edge. My mouth hangs open wide, but not for air. I vomit what feels like gallons of water all over myself and the side of the pool, my torso constricting with each painful expulsion. A wretched cough takes over, ridding my lungs of any residual mist, my organs battered by the violence of the reflex. The gleaming pool winks beneath the security lights as if it was all a game.

The rhythmic clapping sound of the water doesn't mask a louder squelching from the far end of the pool. A long shadow forms against the blue tile walls of the room.

I can't rest – it's found me here, as usual. This routine is beginning to feel as familiar as a heartbeat, but that doesn't make it any less frightening. My feet slap wet prints on the floor as I rush past a sign that says, "No Running." The hell I won't. I let the mysterious pull in my navel guide me out of what I see now is the community center building, and toward home.

Back home, all I want is a shower, to scrub the chemical residue from my skin, thaw in the steam, and rinse this nightmare down the drain.

The floor creaks beneath my tiptoe on my way to the bathroom, and Mom calls into the hallway.

"Kitty? You up?"

I pause outside the bathroom door and cringe, wrapping my arms around myself, shivering in my wet clothes. I can't let her see me looking like this. I can't answer the questions she'd ask, and I don't want to worry her. So, instead of going straight to her room in response, like I'd normally do, I clear my throat and say, "Yeah." I school my voice into nonchalance even as my teeth chatter. "I'm just taking a shower to help me sleep. I was working on a book report and lost track of time. Didn't mean to wake you."

"Oh, okay. Well, goodnight, honey."

"Night, Mom."

Beneath the gentle stream of the shower, so light and different compared to the density of the pool, my muscles thaw and the full reality of the situation hits me. My face crumples and tears run down my cheeks, dripping and mixing into the running water on my body. I almost didn't make it out of that pool. If I'd woken up just seconds later, I could've drowned before the mystery creature even caught up to me. Why is this happening? What did I do to deserve this waking nightmare? No matter how I examine it, I can't figure it out. What's the reasoning behind it? And, most important, how do I make it stop?

CHAPTER 10

RAIN PATTERS on the ceiling above my head the following night, a million tiny fingers tapping on the roof, drumming an impatient tune, probably waiting for me to fall asleep. The rain used to be soothing; I don't know when that changed. Now it's irritating. My blood bubbles like a boiling kettle, fizzing beneath my skin, itching to burst out of my body and spray into the world. I wonder if this is what it's like to be high. I lay in bed beneath the covers, restless, my legs jiggling uncontrollably. It's nearly midnight, and all is quiet in the house. Thunder rumbles, a grumbling of discontent. I wait to see if lightning illuminates my blinds, but it doesn't happen. The storm is still too far away. It's coming, though. I can feel it – the air has shifted into something heavy.

I get up and shake a couple of caffeine pills from the bottle on my desk into my hand, swallowing them with some lukewarm cola.

My lamp flickers and I tense, shoulders scrunched.

Movement near my window catches my attention. I cross the room to inspect and my insides squirm. Maggots crawl along the windowsill, inching steadily over the rim and down the wall. They cross the floor into my room. Why is this still happening?

Maggots can't infest a house like termites, can they? *Where* are they coming from? I stare in disturbed fascination, equally mesmerized and horrified to realize they're coming straight for me in a perfect line. One crawls over my foot and up the leg of my sweatpants, and that's when panic takes over, hot and mindless. I flail about, frantically kicking my leg to shake it out.

A squelchy sound forces me to look up at the window. The blinds are down, but I'm suddenly terrified of what might be on the other side. The sound repeats, reminding me of when Mom eats noodles, slurping up the broth. I try ignoring it, but it's too loud, too obvious *something's* out there. Sucking in a breath for courage, stomach taut and ready for anything, I yank the cord, raising the slats and exposing the glass.

My blood turns to ice in my veins – I am a human slushie. Am I really seeing this, or is this another one of my nightmares? I blink, but it does nothing to dislodge the image in the window. I expected a person, maybe an animal. But this?

A large, formless shape wavers on the other side, yet the sound continues. Dark and shadowy, my wide eyes register what they can while my brain struggles to piece it together: glistening wet texture...the deep, veiny purple of an organ never meant to see light...squishy flesh riddled with zit-sized bumps. Whole face a mouth, gaping and waiting...clearly hungry.

But what does it eat? It slinks down out of sight, and after a few moments of shaky breathing, I summon the courage to step closer to the window, to catch a glimpse of where it's gone. But I'm too slow, too hesitant, and when I peer through the glass, there's nothing to see but the rainy night sky, glowing gray with suburban light.

Am I hallucinating? Is my brain cracking from all the stimulants?

My leg tickles as the maggots, with renewed single focus, crawl up my legs, leaving a slimy trail on my skin. I cry out and drop the blinds before stripping off my pants and shaking them loose. I grab a shoe and slam it down over and over again on the creepy white crawlers. The rug smears with creamy goo, and I swallow the urge to vomit.

A strange noise captures my attention, soft and muffled. The stupid moth is long dead. I've already swept its flaky corpse from the corner of my room. I strain to listen – the silence is more deafening than sound. Wait, there it is again. A cry. That's weird. The only other person here is...

Mom?

I fling a bathrobe over my half-naked body and scurry into the hall.

"Kitty!"

It *is* Mom.

In two seconds, I'm in her room, pausing in the doorway to assess the scene. She's sitting up in bed, panting, but there's no obvious source of her stress. "What's wrong?" I ask.

"My chest," she says, wincing. She rubs below her neck. "It hurts to breathe."

"Oh God." Breathing issues have plagued her since the weight gain, but it's never been this frightening.

"Kitty," she wheezes. Her face blanches as her round cheeks turn purple, a contrast I wouldn't have thought possible. "I can't breathe."

"I'll get help." I run back to my room for my phone – too panicked to think of using hers – and dial 911. They assure me help is on the way and ask a ton of questions about her symptoms. "I don't know," I tell them. My heart beats so fast it practically hums. Hyperventilating, I pant as though I can suck in enough air for the both of us. My eyes dampen with frustrated tears. "She just can't breathe. Please hurry!"

———

The two paramedics can't do much for her other than monitor her situation. The taller one, with a scruffy days' worth of stubble down his neck, averts his eyes. "I'm afraid we can't move you, ma'am," he says. He drops his voice as he addresses me directly, like he's embarrassed. "It appears she's too large for transport to the hospital."

His partner, a woman around Mom's age with a hardened face that shows she means business, keeps checking her pulse, one hand firmly on Mom's wrist, eyes trained on her watch. "We don't have the means to take you," she says briskly. "You simply won't fit." Disgust tinges her raspy smoker's voice, and anger heats my skin. "On the bright side, I don't believe it's a heart attack, even though it might've seemed like one to you. It's just pressure from the excess weight on your lungs. Has your doctor gone over any diets with you lately?"

It's not that simple, you dumb bitch, I want to say. I swallow to keep the bitter words to myself. Mom doesn't need the extra aggravation right now.

"We'll go over it again soon, I'm sure," Mom wheezes.

"That's probably your best bet." The lady paramedic grabs her bag and nods at the tall guy standing by the door, who sheepishly rubs his neck. "Call us again if anything changes."

What would be the point?

After they leave, I curl up at the end of her bed and watch her chest rise and fall as she dozes, making sure it doesn't stop. It could, and that's the scary part.

I smooth away a crease on the blanket, my hand making a whispering sound as it glides over the embroidered material. She grunts and stirs. Her eyes flutter open and land their sleepy gaze on me.

"Hi." I sit up straight, suddenly alert. "How are you feeling?"

She clears her throat. "Some water?"

I jump up and quickly fill her glass from the bedside pitcher. She takes it with both hands trembling, so I support the base with my palm. "There you go," I say as she sips. "Better?"

"Mm-hmmm." She wipes her mouth with the back of her hand, regarding me with a careful expression. "Sorry for the scare, kiddo."

I shrug. "You're okay, that's what matters."

"Even still." She can't hide the humiliation in her eyes. "You shouldn't have to see me like that."

I protest but it's weak. Because she's right. We both know it. She sighs and it's not as deep as I'd like. She rubs her chest as though it aches. It probably does. It probably always will.

She leans her head back against the pillows propped on the headboard. "I feel like a monster, not a human being anymore. My own daughter helps wipe my ass. I've put you through too much. I'm sorry."

I inhale, thinking of the best way to say what needs to be said. "Mom, I've been thinking."

"Oh?"

"This thing that happened today..." Oh God, just say it already. "I need you to listen, okay?"

"Honey."

"I was really, really scared today. I thought I was losing you. It was awful." Way to make it about myself. It was awful for me? What about her? It must have been ten times worse. Why do I mess everything up? I drop my head and briskly rub my face. "Jeez, I'm not saying this right."

I pause and chew the inside of my cheek, gathering my thoughts.

She nods, solemn. "Go on, sweetie."

"I don't want you to die," I blurt out earnestly. "Not like this. It doesn't have to be this way. You're still young, and I need you." I hate bringing this up, especially after how rude the paramedic was, but it must be said. "Remember when the doctor said you need to get... healthier? I think it's time. For real. I can find that worksheet with the arm exercises on it; remember we got it from the nurse that one time? I can help you do them every day if you want. I don't mind. And we can order some portion-controlled meals too. You can rely on me for support. I want to help. Will you do it?" *Please say yes*, I think.

She mulls it over. "I hear what you're saying," she says, "and you're right. I could stand to make some changes. It won't be easy, I know. But... I'm not the only one with problems around here. You have some challenges to overcome as well."

My head goes fuzzy with heat. It's one thing for me to recognize my issues. But when someone else points it out? Toe-curling shame sweeps through my body. Is this how I made her feel? I'm regretting even starting this conversation. "Like what?"

"You know exactly what I'm talking about."

"Care to elaborate?"

"You're a smart girl, so don't play fool with me. You never go out. Period. You think that's a good way to live?"

"Well, no, I guess not..."

"Right, so we both need to make some changes. I'll work on losing the weight and you'll work on your anxiety. Agreed?"

Did she just flip the switch on me? My heart sinks, weighed down with sadness. "You aren't willing to get better without an ultimatum?"

"It would be easier knowing we're both getting better. Together. Can you understand?"

"But there's nothing wrong with me!" Even as I say it, I know it's a lie.

"Oh, but my darling, there is."

I'm speechless. "I'll – I'll have to think about it."

In my room, I thump my mattress with my foot. How dare she? Her life is in actual, imminent danger – she could have a heart attack or a stroke at any second – and she questions *my* lifestyle? All I have to worry about is staying inside. I settle at my desk and open my laptop, prepared to bash out a long, furious diary post – but then I stop. My shoulders slump in defeat. Deep down in the place inside me that I don't want to admit exists, I know she speaks the truth.

Maybe the only way to stop the disappearing at night and the *thing* in the window is to face the world head on. Prove that I am capable of living like a typical person. I think of Janelle, how she's offered to support me on my first time out in years. She's just waiting for me to make the call.

If I don't do this, Mom will only get worse.

I grab my phone and text Janelle one word, practically stabbing the screen with my fingertips: *fine*. Maybe if I do this, Mom will realize how serious I am, though my body has gone numb from the decision.

A minute later, my phone buzzes with an incoming call.

"Awesome!" Janelle is over the moon. I have never seen her so animated. "I can't wait. Your first excursion in forever, and we finally get to meet!"

"But why does it have to be a gross, scary Halloween thing? Why can't we go someplace, like, quiet?"

"Theaters are quiet. No talking allowed."

"Until the scream queens get their shriek on."

"That's just part of the fun. You need to get your heart pumping; make you feel alive."

If she only knew. "My heart's doing enough of that already, thanks very much."

She laughs and it's a deep, full-bellied sound. The kind that would be contagious and have me giggling with her if I weren't so petrified about what I've agreed to do.

CHAPTER 11

THINGS WEREN'T VERY good in our house after Dad left. I had my speculations as to why he walked away, and most of it had to do with my neurosis. But I never let myself think about how Mom lost her shit too. It all comes back now.

A few months after my second failed attempt at staying home alone, Mom came home from the store, empty-handed, bloody, and shaken. Someone with a gun stole her purse right off her and knocked her to the ground. The way she told us made me feel like I was living it with her. I saw it the way she must've seen it, the weapon glinting in the yellowish light of the parking lot, skin turned clammy, and knees weakened with fear, knowing that at any second a bullet would end it all.

I handed her a box of tissues to clean the blood from her chin, scraped by pavement. What more could I do?

Weeks turned into months, and she could only find solace in food. I'm not sure I noticed too much, being a kid and all – I was too wrapped up in my own battles.

Dad tried soothing her the best he could, I guess. He understood, I think, at least for a little while. According to all the websites, traumatic events take time to heal. And she needed time to recover, like I did. But maybe my issues made it harder for him to be patient with us. One agoraphobe was plenty. But then Mom didn't want to go out either and, for a time, I had a partner indoors.

We'd regularly settle in together on the couch with pizza and ice cream and funny movies, finding temporary release in predictably scripted, well-timed comedic relief. Movie night was the only time our laughter filled the house. We got each other for once. I felt validation for my desire to be at home. If Mom wanted it too, then it must be okay, right?

The only thing was, Dad wasn't totally on board. At first, he was gentle in his persuasion. He used subtlety and genuine concern to get her some help. "Set an example for our daughter," I once heard him say through the walls. He didn't know I could hear them. I was torn between wanting to eavesdrop and putting the pillow over my head. "She's already struggling with problems, and here you are, encouraging her damaging behavior. None of this is healthy, for either of you. How do you think this is affecting her? Her hibernation's getting out of control, and, honey, no offense, but I'm worried about your physical health. This isn't going to help you in the long run, you know?"

"Fuck you," Mom spat, and I recoiled, having never heard her use that word before, let alone as a direct curse to my father. My heart shriveled as they argued and fought about who was right and who was wrong and, after a while, I buried my head beneath my pillow and bit back a scream. The outside world was too dangerous, and my inside world was falling apart. Nothing could be trusted. I wasn't safe anywhere.

Turns out Mom wasn't safe either, but it wasn't external forces we should've worried about. It was herself. One night while Dad and I slept, she went out to face her fears.

She walked. For miles. Alone in the dark. To this day I wonder if she was tempting fate on purpose, proving to herself that it was safe, that nothing would happen, or if she knew where her feet were leading all along. I never asked, never really wanted to know her answer – count that as another one of my fears.

There's a long bridge that connects our neighborhood to the bustling downtown area where all the shops and restaurants are. A construction of metal and stone arching across the Wildrood River divides our town in half, simultaneously imposing and quaint. Somehow, Mom ended up on that bridge. She doesn't go into detail about that night and what happened, but I imagine her there, shivering in her nightgown, as she leaned over the edge, watching the rushing river below. We will never know what was in her mind when she climbed up onto the balustrade, balancing on the rim, toeing the edge. When she jumped, I imagine she simply tilted forward and let gravity do the work. I wonder if she felt free, like a bird.

I don't think about the seconds afterward, the impact, her body literally coming back to earth, the pain, the panic, the sheer terror of onlookers and passersby. I'm grateful to the quick-thinking person that swam in after her and saved her life, and the others that called for an ambulance and stayed by her side until help arrived.

She lived, thank God, but not without injuries. The doctor said her fall was "just right" for avoiding head trauma, but her left leg and wrist were broken on impact. Now she had an excuse to lie around the house while her leg healed, and that might have been Dad's tipping point. I don't think he ever forgave her for trying to leave us. That's a certain kind of heartbreak I bury in housework, cooking, school assignments for extra credit, and games. Unfortunately, Dad didn't have obsessions to cushion the blow. When he left, Mom cried for ages. I held her, and we cried together, her leg immobilized by a hard cast, and that's likely the exact moment she stopped getting out of bed. When I remember it, it all leads back to that day. Sometimes I wonder if I could've fixed myself, made myself better so he'd want to stay at least for one of us. But he chose to leave us both, so I no longer allow him space in my head.

That's why this is so hard. Mom and I have both spiraled so

far out of control that digging our way out of our collective ruts is going to be tough.

———————

Baby steps. Change doesn't happen overnight. "You can do it, kiddo!" Mom calls from her room. I stand on our front stoop, phone in hand. The milliseconds whiz by on the stopwatch. My eyes squeeze shut. I can do this, I can.

It's not like I don't go outside *ever*. Janelle might've been teasing before, but she was right; I do get the mail and stuff. Our bills are online so most of it's junk, like coupons for driveway blacktop or whatever. I usually wait a few days to let the crap build up, then dart out to the box and run back inside as quickly as possible, dumping the colorful papers in the recycling bin on the way. Twelve seconds flat. Easy-peasy.

Mom set a goal for me today. She told me to take my time, not rush. Stroll to the mailbox as if I haven't a care in the world. No limit, just slow down a little. The cold breeze dances through the trees and kisses my face – it smells of dead leaves and mulch. Our yard is overgrown with dying grass and thick, invasive weeds. Dad used to keep it nice and tidy when he was around, the headache-inducing rumble and gasoline scent of the lawn mower filling the air each summer weekend. Not anymore.

The neighbor's Jack-o-lanterns across the street stare at me, frozen in anticipation – *will the freak actually do it?* I clutch the door handle behind my back as the world spins. Other people do this all the time. Why do I have to be the broken one?

One. Two. Three. A single step. Then another. I can't feel the door behind me now. My gaze skitters up and down the street. A lone car cruises by, the driver looking down at the phone in his hand. God, what if he veered off the road and hit me? I shake my head. Keep counting.

Four. Five.

I'm down the steps now, on the footpath. Gray circular stones act as functional decoration, a throwback to fairytale cottages in the stories my parents would read me at bedtime. The long grass creeps over the edges of the stones, touching my shoes.

More than halfway to the mailbox, Kit, slow down.

I stand still in the middle of the yard, taking it all in. My surroundings. The environment. Nature. Life. Kids laugh in the distance, playing some game, but I can't see which house it's coming from. The sound echoes inside my skull, bouncing around like the pellet of a pinball machine. I roll my shoulders, tense. I have to relax, even if I'm only faking it to myself. Relax.

I saunter to the mailbox as if I don't have a care, pop the metal lip, pull the door open, and it squeaks, a long metallic cry. I never actually noticed how loud it is. Should it be oiled or something? Another car goes by. Faster than the last one. A steel torpedo, the rush of air lifts the hem of my cardigan. I choke on exhaust, the metallic flavor coating my tongue. My heart trills, reverberating against the edges of my skull. My ribcage tightens, lungs cinching like I've put on an ill-fitting corset. My mouth opens and closes like a fish, desperate for air. A small part of my brain understands that I'm breathing just fine but tell that to my body. It's not getting the memo, and panic sets in.

No, I can't do this. I don't even bother getting the mail; I leave the box hanging open, its contents exposed for the whole neighborhood to see. I run to the house, slamming the door behind me. Check the stopwatch.

Thirty-two seconds. And I didn't even get the mail. Shit. If I can't make this happen, how will I ever survive a trip to the movies?

Mom says it's a good start, that it's all about mindfulness and intention. "I'm just proud of you for trying."

I take her compliments, but deep down I'm concerned. A week has passed, and even though I'm trying, she hasn't followed through on her part of the deal. Oh, sure, she waved her arms a few times and called it exercise, but it's been a few days, and she hasn't done it again. I give her smaller portions at mealtimes, and she complains so much about hunger that I feel obligated to give her more. But she doesn't want more peas or broccoli – she wants bread, chips, and cookies. If I don't give in to her, she gets angry and pouts. Tension bubbles up between us, thick like cheese in a casserole, and I hate that, so I usually cave in to her cravings and give her what she wants. It doesn't seem like she's working as hard as I am, and I don't know how much longer this can go on.

CHAPTER 12

JANELLE DRIVES a clunky Toyota so old that it was probably black once but has since faded to the color of a storm cloud. The metal body's banged up like it's seen its fair share of accidents, making me second-guess this whole thing. As she pulls up to the curb in front of my house, I drop the curtain and back away from Mom's window. "I can't do this," I say, my voice tight. My lungs won't expand properly, the muscles around my ribcage cramping in a tight spasm – I might be having another panic attack.

"You can." Mom lowers the volume on her TV. "Breathe, darling. Like a balloon, no hurry. In... and out." She demonstrates the slow breathing technique we learned in a video, and I mimic her. It's a struggle, but eventually my muscles loosen, and I suck in an adequate amount of oxygen. "Okay. I'm good now."

"Yes, you are, girl. Now go have fun." She turns the volume back up – some show about husbands cheating with nannies or whatever. I kiss her head and move toward the door where I linger, clutching my purse. It's a cheap, faux leather thing I forgot I even had. It was a Christmas gift some years ago from a grandparent I barely remember. I don't know whether to carry it in my hands or sling it over my shoulder. "I have my phone," I assure her.

"You won't need it," she says. "This is your time. Now get out of here."

"As I live and breathe," Janelle says on my doorstep. "If it isn't Kit Hoffman in the actual flesh."

I tuck a strand of hair behind my ear. "Hello to you too."

"So, not a catfish. Cool. Can I pinch you? Make sure you're real?"

"I'd rather you not."

We grin like idiots, reveling in the moment. I wondered if it would be awkward, but all our time online together has solidified our relationship, and being around her feels as natural as breathing. This is simply an extension of our late-night chats. Aside from Mom, she's the only person in this world who truly knows me. She doesn't force a hug or anything, just lightly touches my shoulder as if to check I'm not a hologram or some shit, and the warmth from her fingertips light me up inside.

My smile fades as we head to her car. I'm actually doing this. *This* is real.

Janelle watches with uncontained amusement as I struggle with the seat belt. "Oh. My. God." She snickers, putting a hand to her mouth. Her eyes crinkle, betraying her silent laughter.

"Shut up," I grunt, yanking the woven nylon strap repeatedly. "It's been a while." The stupid thing won't stretch. Isn't it supposed to glide? It suddenly jerks forward with my full body-weight, and I nearly slam my head into the dashboard. My cheeks redden, and Janelle doesn't hide her laughter anymore. It's been years since I've been in a car – obviously I never got my driver's license – and I'd almost forgotten how seat belts work. How embarrassing. But that's not the only seemingly inconsequential thing I've forgotten. The vibration of the engine rattles my bones, sort of like when I lean against the dryer. I'd forgotten the invisible force that pins me back as the car accelerates, how the world blurs, and how narrow the road looks through the windshield. Does Janelle notice these things, or has she become used to them? I don't think I ever realized how trapped we are inside a moving vehicle. You might think that's something I'd actually like about driving, but I'm petrified we'll crash, and our bodies will twist, snap, and smear the cracked plastic-leather seats with our guts. I don't want to get buried in this steel coffin. I play it cool for Janelle, even as my skin goes clammy, and I close my eyes when she isn't looking.

The cinema isn't far. Only about seven minutes from my house. I hadn't realized how close it was this whole time. Everything seems far away when you're a kid, so I guess my sense of distance is kind of distorted these days. Thankfully the seat belt is easier to release than to draw, and I avoid making a spectacle of myself getting out of the car. The crisp air is tinged with smells both foreign and familiar. Memories of childhood spring to mind, of drive-through restaurants and fast-food fries. Yes, we get junk food delivered no-contact from time to time, but it's not really in our budget, and the fries are always soggy by the time they arrive. And baking frozen potatoes in the oven just doesn't have the same effect. I've been taunted for years by advertisements of hot, fresh, grease-laden fries, crisped to perfection in a deep fryer. My mouth waters. Could I suggest we skip the movie in favor of McDonald's? We could sit in the car and stuff our faces with food I never get to eat anymore. And if all goes well...well. One thing at a time.

"I hope you didn't look up any reviews," Janelle says, coming around the front of the car. "You can't trust those pretentious film crits. They don't understand the art of campy horror."

"I didn't, don't worry."

"Good." She shoves her hands deep in the pockets of her navy puffer vest. Her eyes sparkle in the cold. "You ready?"

I gaze up at the brick building looming over the parking lot. A sea of vehicles lie between us and it. Trepidation crawls up my spine, a sensation of marching spiders, a hundred pointy legs.

"I'll be right here with you. There's nothing to be scared of."

Easy for her to say. She doesn't know for sure. Nevertheless, we're here. I bite my lip and nod.

She grins. "Okay then. Let's go."

I follow her through the parking lot, taking note of groups of clustered teenagers. They occasionally shout greetings or obscenities to each other – it's kind of hard to tell the difference. My muscles tighten. Every step I take is short and awkward. I feel like a toddler inching my way across the blacktop. Janelle patiently walks beside me, whispering encouraging words the whole time. I inhale the delicious air and exhale slow, like Mom said. It takes longer than I imagine it would for a normal person, but we eventually make it to the wide, revolving glass doors, which usher us inside. "I did it," I say, breathless. "I'm here. I'm at the movies. Holy crap."

"I'm so fuckin' proud of you!" Janelle squeezes my hands.

I gaze at my surroundings, taking it all in. Being anywhere other than home is sort of overwhelming. The sights, the sounds, the odors – buttered popcorn and warm sweat – I clench my fists and try grounding into the blood-red carpet. Velvet curtains frame the doorways, giving the illusion of grandeur. But dust coats the massive ruffles...ruffles that a madman – or a wormy shadow – could hide behind. I see the stains on the carpet, presumably from spilled sodas and muck tracked in from the lot – or blood from a knife fight long forgotten. The popcorn maker punctures the atmosphere with machine-gun fire, putting my nerves on edge. I grit my teeth and try to remember why I'm doing this. It's healthy. It's fun.

So, when does the fun actually start?

"And this is my treat – no, really, I already bought the tickets – your reward for being so brave." She squeezes my arm. "It's so good to see you, like, for real. I'm glad you came."

"Thanks, yeah. Me too."

"Popcorn?"

Pop, pop, pop. Gunpowder fills my brain. "Sure."

The line for concessions isn't very long, but I find myself huddling closer to Janelle than necessary. We get two large buckets with extra butter and ice-cold Cokes. The drinks come in ginormous plastic cups splashed with images of the latest superhero flick. I stab a straw through the lid and take a long sip to steady my nerves. Janelle's already pounding her popcorn, and we haven't even approached the ticket taker yet. As she juggles her snacks with one hand, she pulls up the ticket app with the other.

My purse vibrates against my hip. My phone.

"Hang on. Can you take this a sec?" I hand her my cup and unsnap my purse. She looks mildly annoyed, like I'm about to run off or something. "What's up?"

"I just – my phone's ringing." I clasp my fingers around it, the buzz rattling my knuckles.

"I know it's been a while since you've been here," she says, "but you know you'll have to silence that, right?"

"Yeah, yeah, no problem." I check the name and my heart liquefies, slithering to my stomach. It's Mom. Everything darkens around me. All I can see is her name on the screen. She could just be calling to check up on me, to make sure I'm having a good time. That's what moms do, right? She said she wouldn't, but maybe she changed her mind.

Janelle peers at my face. "You okay?"

I hold up the phone. "I gotta take this. Sorry." I walk a few paces away from the turnstiles and stand next to a life-size cutout of Jennifer Lawrence. "Mom? Mom, are you there?"

Silence. A sour taste floods my mouth.

"Mom, is everything alright?"

A gasp. Then, so quiet I almost miss it, "Kitty?"

It's a weird sense of reverse déjà vu. Is this what it was like when I called her that first time all those years ago? Did someone break in again? Did she hurt herself again? Why do these things keep repeating?

"Mom, I'm coming back now. Right now. I'll be there as soon as I can. Don't hang up, okay?" I face Janelle with wide eyes. "You have to take me back now. It's my mom."

"Is she okay?"

"I don't know." My throat dries up. "I don't think so."

"Okay. Come on, we're leaving." She dumps our snacks in the nearest bin and hustles me out of the theater.

My phone's pressed tight to my ear, but Mom's still quiet. What's wrong with her? "She's not talking," I explain to Janelle as we rush to the car. Adrenaline propels me across the parking lot at a speed I never thought possible, even after all these nights getting chased. Tears slide down my cheeks, hot and salty as they seep between my lips.

The car races through the streets, and I don't even mind the jolting turns around corners and speeding through yellow lights. The faster the better. Mom needs me.

CHAPTER 13

"MOM?" I burst into the house with Janelle on my heels. I don't think about how long it's been since someone other than family and paramedics has been here, or how strange it is the way the energy shifts with her presence. I'm super embarrassed – it's like a spotlight beaming directly on our delusions, on display for her to see. Her nose scrunches for a second – only a second – and I think of the smell, how thick it must be for someone unused to it. Shame warms my face, but I can't think of that now. I run straight to Mom's room. She's in bed where I left her, naturally, and she makes a weird gargling sound as if choking. But I didn't leave any food in her room – so what could be wrong?

"Mom, what is it?"

She clutches her chest as if to claw out her own heart. I rush to her side and scatter my gaze up and down her body, trying to pinpoint anything visibly wrong other than her lack of breath. She's clearly struggling. "My – *gasp* – chest," she wheezes. Her voice is thin, brittle, and reedy. "Can't – *gasp* – breathe."

"Call 911, okay?" I shout at Janelle. But she doesn't have to answer – her phone's already to her ear, and I've never been more grateful to have her as a friend. I'm listening as she relays information to the operator. "I'm not sure," she says. "Here's her daughter." She hands the phone to me.

"Ma'am," the dispatch operator says. His voice is maddeningly calm. "Can you describe the symptoms?"

"I – I don't know, she just can't breathe. She's a bariatric patient, this happened before. But it's worse now."

"Do you know her exact weight?"

"Um..." Honestly, it's been so long since she's been on a scale, I don't know. Based on her previous reading, though, I can certainly guess. It's not a number I like saying out loud. "Just shy of eight was our last estimate. It's definitely more now." Janelle's eyes go wide. I shake my head and focus on Mom.

"Eight hundred?" he asks. To his credit, his tone remains neutral.

"Yeah, maybe."

I'm assured help is on the way. "Please make them hurry," I whisper, watching the color drain from Mom's face. My fear for her life overrides my fear of people entering my home. "They're coming," I tell her, rubbing wide circles on her back in the hope that it will encourage her lungs to relax and soften. But it's not her lungs causing the problem – it's the excess fat pressing down on her organs, making it harder for them to work properly. I hold back tears. The salt makes my eyes sting, but I refuse to let them fall. I must be strong now.

Janelle waits by the front door and lets the paramedics in with their crisp uniforms and professional "we got this" demeanor. They're not the same ones as before, but I'm still worried this'll be a repeat of last time. Will they tell us it's a false alarm and to maybe have some carrots for dinner?

They approach Mom whose eyes flutter, eerily rolling back in her head. She must be getting faint. "Ma'am? We're here to help. What's your name?"

She rasps. "Marybeth. *Gasp.* Hoffman."

"Great. Marybeth, you're having some trouble breathing?"

Obviously. She doesn't respond. "We found her like this," I

explain. I chew my thumbnail as they try taking her blood pressure, but the cuff doesn't fit. "We'll need a thigh cuff for her arm," one guy mumbles into a walkie talkie. "Radio ahead for a bariatric lift."

They ask me about her health history, her medications. They ask me twice how much she weighs. Can't they hurry up and help her already? She looks so miserable, and I'm standing here, helpless, as they pepper us with questions. They seemed so capable when they first arrived, so confident in their dark blue uniforms, covered in reflective stripes and official patches.

They came in with a stretcher, but now it leans against the wall, unused. There's no way Mom would fit. And that scares me the most. If she needs emergency assistance outside of this house, how will she get it? I press my knuckles hard on my lips to keep from crying. I'm horrified by that thought but more by what it could ultimately mean. I always knew this was a potentially lethal problem. Not really a matter of if, but when. How do you bring that up to a parent? How do you tell the person that raised you they need to change, that they're messing up, that you're scared they'll leave you before it's time? Things could've been different. If she'd handled her fear in a better way, seen a therapist, taken up a self-defense class, or journaled, would that have made a difference? Instead, she became a shut-in and ate.

The similarities are not lost on me. Is this the path I'm also headed down?

I'm not skinny, by any means, but I'm not at Mom's level either. I could be, if I'm not careful. It's as if a curtain lifts from my eyes and I'm seeing clearly what should've been obvious to me all this time. I've been a hypocrite. She tried warning me. We're the same, Mom and me, and it's time to make a change. But how? I spin around, looking for something to do to help, but there's nothing. I look at the bed, and my heart constricts. Darting my gaze away, it lands on her nightstand and the bible laying there next to her tumbler and a half empty box of tissues. I move toward it and touch the textured leather cover. Please, God, let her live. I'm not very religious, but if Mom makes it through, I'll be good, I'll start praying and reading my own bible with the gilded pages that Grandma Hoffman sent me one Christmas. I'll stop cursing and reading smutty fanfiction, I promise.

They give her oxygen and wait to see if her condition worsens. There's not much else they can do. Seeing her like that, vulnerable, with a plastic mask over her face is ghastly and heartbreaking. My heart crumbles as I put on a brave face. She needs support right now, not a bawling baby.

Sirens pierce the air outside. A second ambulance has come. I imagine the neighbors gathering out front, whispering, curious. The new set of paramedics have brought a contraption that's supposed to help get Mom into the ambulance. It looks scary though, all black straps and gray buckles. "It's okay, Mom, I'm right here." I squeeze her hand. Her grip is weak. "Please hurry," I urge them.

They talk amongst themselves outside the bedroom door. One guy with a buzz cut looks really frustrated, and the other, a short, squat kid probably not much older than me, appears super confused. He keeps scratching at the back of his head, looking like a child playing make-believe at a grown-up job. His uniform could just as well be a costume. I catch the words "problem" and "too big." I stroke Mom's arm and tell her I'll be right back.

I approach the medics with trepidation. "What's going on? Why aren't you taking her?"

"Uh..." The confused kid won't meet my eyes. Buzz Cut doesn't beat around the bush, reminding me a little of the rude woman who couldn't help her before. "Your mother's too big to move."

The words cut to my core. Warm slush churns in my stomach as guilt. I did this to her. I enabled her. "But I thought that weird thing you guys brought would help."

"It would, if only we could fit her through the door."

I look at Mom and then the door. Our house is on the older side, before open plan living was a thing, and the doorways are smaller, I suppose, than ones in a newer build. Truth is, she's been room-bound for so long it never occurred to me that she can't squeeze through the narrow frame anymore.

"Oh," I say, dismayed.

"We could, possibly, remove the frame to widen it."

Break the door? Seriously?

"I can't see any other way. Either that or we just wait and see what happens. But if it's special equipment or surgery she needs, she'll have to be at the hospital."

Surgery? My ears go fuzzy and my mind spins. Every second counts. We're wasting time talking about this. "Do it." My words sound muffled inside my head. "Whatever you have to do."

They call in additional manpower, and it's agony waiting for them to arrive with the tools. I stand back in disbelief as grown men tear apart my house. First, the doorframe to the bedroom. The wall crumbles, revealing its guts of fluffy pink insulation. It takes longer than I'd like. Then they work on our sliding back door, which puts up more of a structural fight. But they say it's easier than damaging the front door. They break the seam and remove the sheets of glass. The whole process is tedious, loud, and excruciating to watch.

The actual transport is worse. Mom groans the whole time, obviously in pain the way her face pinches up. They talk to her, a steady stream of encouragement, keeping her engaged.

I'm not allowed to ride with them because there isn't room. Janelle offers to drive. "Come on, Kit, I'll take you." She jingles the keys in her hand. I can't believe she stayed for all of this.

The room spins. I'm torn. This is all too much – this roller coaster of a day has ruined me. I shake my head.

"I need to stay and watch the house." I glance at the back door. The extra guys that came to help are working as quickly as they can to reinstall it. But if they could take it down in the first place, lock be damned, what's to stop others from doing the same? How can they guarantee no one will break in during the night? I might as well put a sign out back saying Enter Here.

"I can stay with you, if you want," she says. But I can't have her witness any more of this. I'm so humiliated.

"No, it's okay. Thanks."

I send her home with promises of updates. I curl up on the couch, feeling like I've aged a hundred years. If there's a silver lining to this awfulness, it's that I'll never be able to sleep. I'm too worried about Mom, the vulnerability of the house, and what Janelle must think of me now.

I stay up the whole night.

CHAPTER 14

IN THE DARK, early hour of the morning, I'm on the brink of dozing off, but something jolts me back to full consciousness. The table lamp glows next to me, the bulb fading and brightening. I'm curled in the fetal position and slowly unkink myself, stretching my coiled muscles until my joints pop. I rub my neck. It's sore – I've been lying with it cricked at a funny angle.

A collective "ooh" followed by applause meets my ear.

I bolt upright.

The TV's on. A late-night infomercial host plays up to an overly enthusiastic audience the many benefits of owning the latest set of frying pans. I left it off to better hear if anyone messed with the doorway. Maybe I rolled over the remote or something. But no, the remote's on the coffee table, an arm's reach away. Tentatively I grab it and jab the power button. With a mild electronic pop, the TV goes dark.

Something feels off. I'm prompted to get up and check the back door. I examine all around its edges to be sure it's securely in place.

Rubbing the goosebumps from my arms, I turn up the thermostat. It's way too cold in here. I get a hoodie from my room and pull it over my head, relishing the extra layer of warmth. I think about Mom and my heart lurches, the muscles stretching, reaching for her, wishing to be near her...how can I complain about a little sweater weather when she's in the hospital being poked and prodded? She might even be too big for surgery, and then her fate will be sealed. I'm petrified my phone will ring. On one hand, I want news. On the other, it could be devastating. I have to work up the nerve to go see her, but I'm torn between my love for her and fear of what could happen if I leave.

Muffled laughter carries out of Mom's room, floating down the hallway. My skin prickles. What's going on?

I walk over to her room, grimacing at the battered wall where the doorframe should be, the rough edges a grisly reminder of the hell we're living in. Her TV is on now, a game show, the host charming the contestants with too-white teeth and too much charisma. The remote isn't in its usual spot on the bedside table. I shut my eyes, holding back tears. I'm too freaked out to step into the room, but I have to turn it off. Holding my breath, staying quiet, I tiptoe inside the room. Looking around for the remote, I spot it on the floor, halfway under her bed. What made it fall? Most likely it got knocked there earlier, during the chaos. But how did the TV turn itself on? And why?

My phone rings and I jump. Even though I'd been hoping for it, there's something eerie about getting a call at this hour. An unknown number lights up the screen. Is it the hospital? Is something wrong with Mom? I swallow a lump. "Hello?"

"Your name has been selected..." A robotic voice tells me to deliver all my personal details if I want to collect the tickets for a cruise I just won, despite never entering a raffle. I hang up. I hate spam calls, but my heart sinks knowing I'll have to keep waiting for news.

I grab the remote and point it at the TV, aiming straight for a giggly blonde about to win a prize, and click off. It stays on. I try again. Same thing. The audience cheers and applauds as if my struggle entertains them. I check the batteries in case they got knocked loose during the fall, but they're all in place. Maybe they're dead. Dropping the remote onto the bed, I march up to the TV and turn it off manually. It finally goes dark, and the house is quiet again.

That was weird, right? Two TVs on simultaneously? What would cause that? A power surge? Wouldn't the lights be affected too? With nervous fingers, I experiment with the light switch, flipping it on and off. Light. Dark. Light. Dark. No problems. I rub my eyes. Maybe I'm just too tired, drained from everything that's happened in the last twelve hours. "Relax," I say out loud. My voice sounds too big for the space. "Just be calm. It's no big deal. Don't freak out over nothing."

A thumping sound freezes my blood.

I face the hallway, pinpricks rippling down my spine. I'm too chicken to explore. I think of the face in the polish, the maggots, the giant *thing* in the window, but this is real; this sounds human. What are the odds *another* person has stumbled into my house? Maybe all the commotion earlier drew the attention of unsavory types, and they watched and waited 'til I was alone to breech the now weakened entrance. I won't call out to them – I've seen too many movies where the victim says "hello?" and reveals their location to the killer. Instead, I creep slowly into the hall. My ears strain to figure out which direction the sound came from, but it doesn't happen again. What the hell? I tiptoe to the living room and pause in the archway, every nerve ending fired, alert to danger. If I'd left the TVs on, would I have even heard it? A low, slow creaking meets my ears. Floorboards dipping beneath someone's weight. A sound I recognize.

But I haven't taken a step.

I peer into the living room.

"Hey."

It's only Janelle, and my limbs dissolve like gelatin powder in hot water. "You scared the shit out of me! How could you?"

"Sorry." She holds up her hands. "I didn't know if you were sleeping, and I didn't want to wake you if you were."

"Well, you would've with all the noise you're making." My

fear has given some bite to my words. I know I'm being unfair; I'm just so worked up. This could've been so much worse.

"Sorry! I bumped my shin on your end table when I took my coat off. My bangles got stuck in the sleeve, and it was kind of a battle." She rattles the spiky bracelets on her wrist.

Something occurs to me. "How did you get in?"

"It was open." She gestures to the front door.

What? I didn't lock it? My tongue dries and turns fuzzy. "Like, *open* open? Not just unlocked?"

"Yeah. It was cracked. Must not have closed all the way or something."

I stare at her, mind swirling. But I did close it. I turned the lock, like always. I take a shaky breath. "What are you doing here anyway?"

"Couldn't sleep." She shrugs. "I'm worried about you. This was some tough shit."

I shrug, unable to play brave any longer.

"How's your mom? I never got an update."

"She's there. And I'm here. It's a waiting game."

"Surgery?"

"Dunno. She's pretty heavy, like you saw. It might not be safe to cut into her until she loses weight. But she could die before that happens." A tear slips loose, betraying my feelings. I need to see her, but I can't even visit my own mother. I'm a selfish failure. "I'm so scared."

"Shh, it's okay, come here." She wraps me in a hug, warm and strange. She smells of sandalwood oil and citrus-flavored energy drinks. I'm taken aback by the gesture – I haven't been hugged by anyone for a while, not even Mom. It's weird but also kind of nice. I don't know what to do with my hands, so I pat her back, feeling the knobs of her spine beneath her soft, cotton top. She holds me for a long minute while I soak her shoulder with quiet tears.

"Oh, I got snot on your shirt," I say, sniffling. "Sorry."

"It's nothing. What's a little booger at a time like this?"

I'm glad she's here. I make us hot coffee with extra cream and real sugar, not the fake diet stuff, and settle on the couch for a movie to pass the time. We have very different taste in films. She likes action with lots of explosions and guts flying everywhere. I prefer gentler comedies. We compromise with a romantic thriller. My mind isn't on the movie though. It's with Mom. As the leading lady runs through a dark alleyway, reminding me of my nighttime chases minus the clicking high heels, I turn to Janelle. "If I ask you a favor," I say, "will you help me?"

"Duh, you nut job. I'm here for you, in case I haven't made that clear enough."

"I need to see Mom. She must be so lonely and scared...if she's even awake that is. Oh God." My heart feels like a boxing bag, punched with hope and guilt and fear and sadness. How long will it take for the inner bruises to appear on my skin? "Once it's light out, I need you to help me get there. And...stay there. I know that's asking a lot."

"No, it's not."

"It might be hard. I'll probably fight you."

"That's okay – I'll win."

"I don't want to resent you for it, even though it's my idea."

"It'd be fine if you did. Worth it, even. I'm behind you on this."

"Really? You'll do it?"

"Duh. You made it to the movies, after all." She chuckles softly and ruffles my hair like a kid. "Silly."

My lips attempt a weak smile. "Thanks."

"We could go right now."

I shake my head. She doesn't know about the shadowy, maggoty creature in the dark. I should tell her. She wouldn't judge. But the words won't come. They stick in my throat like peanut butter. "No," I say weakly. "Not just yet. When it's light."

———

I watch Janelle sleep with mild jealousy. She's curled up like a cat in the armchair, and the knit throw tucked under her chin absorbs a string of drool. How nice it would be to let go like that, to sink into the bliss of sleep. But I stay strong. I can't disappear right now. Getting to Mom is too important. I can't risk being caught by the thing in the shadows.

When sunlight peeks through the blinds and warms the windows, we're buckling up in her car again.

This time, I don't fumble with the seat belt.

This time, I'm prepared for the strange sensations of zipping down highways.

This time, we don't even make it to our destination.

CHAPTER 15

I'M NOT sure what we hit. All I know is that one minute I'm watching Janelle wave a thank you in the rearview mirror – a fellow driver let her cut in front of him – and the next my head snaps forward and back, my torso immobilized by the seat belt. To think I'd hated that strip of nylon – now, I'm grateful for it. It's so fast that I'm not even sure what happened. Based on the loud crunching noise the car made, and the fact we're no longer moving, it makes sense we've been in an accident – a bad one.

"Oh God, oh God." Is that me or Janelle speaking? It's me. My voice is high and tight. I clear my throat, wincing as my skin pulls with the action. My hands shake. Am I injured? Are we hurt?

Movement in the rearview mirror catches my attention, and my heart freezes. The car behind us nearly slams into our bumper. Their tires squeal deafeningly as it fishtails to a stop.

Panicked, I turn to Janelle. Blood dribbles from her forehead – the windshield is cracked where she must've slammed it. Why didn't her seat belt keep her in place? It hangs loose around her hips, stretched to capacity. Was it always like that? I'm not sure I noticed. Her eyes are closed. "Shit."

The driver behind us gets out and knocks on Janelle's window. He's dressed in a business suit, probably headed to work at this time of morning before we interrupted his commute. "Hey," he says. "You okay?"

I can't respond. I don't know the answer. Are we okay? Is he angry? He was being so nice letting us get in front, and this is how we repay him – by causing a wreck. How did this happen? The road stretches long before us – nothing that I can see we hit. No tree, or fence, or building. Was it an animal? But how would that stop the car? It feels like we hit something huge and solid, but we're stopped in the middle of a clear lane.

"I've dialed an ambulance," he's saying. "Just hold tight."

Do emergency services have a loyalty program? I should start earning points. My thoughts are soft, mushy. Do I have a concussion? Whiplash? Will I be taken to the hospital? If an ambulance is coming, they can take me straight to Mom, right? This is just a bump in the road – no pun intended – on the way to my original destination. So why not let them take me there?

Janelle still hasn't opened her eyes. I touch her arm, but my vision blurs. My stomach roils, and I vomit rancid, foamy bile all over myself. I glance up in time to see a black cat standing in the middle of the road, staring at me with otherworldly green eyes. The eyes roll back in its head as it yawns...and keeps yawning until its mouth, full of needle-like teeth, replaces its entire face. The face then stretches long and wide, and it's the mouth from my window. Is this the same thing that's been following me at night? My heart chills, my breath quick and shallow. Does the man not see it? Did *it* cause this? But it's morning. It shouldn't be here. I blink and the mouth-for-a-head disappears. The cat is normal again. It turns and casually walks to the side of the road where it crawls into the ditch and out of sight.

Sirens in the distance. There's an ambulance coming. I fumble with the door handle – my fingers seem flimsy, struggling to grip – and push it open. "Whoa, hold on there," the other driver says. "You should stay put. You're bleeding."

I am? I look down. He's right. My arms are covered in bright red blood, fresh and mineral smelling. On TV it looks either like strawberry or barbecue sauce. In real life, not so much. It's more complex, the reds somehow redder, the texture stickier than I'd realized. "Oh jeez," I mumble, watching the blood ooze and drip from my skin. My head spins, and I blink to steady my gaze, which blurs. I turn my head to look at the watercolor version of Janelle. And that's the last thing I remember.

———

The scratches on my arms and face came from shards of the broken windshield but aren't bad enough for stitches. A few plasters do the trick. The doctor checks me over and declares me fit. My fainting was likely a stress response, not a sign of anything major. But he doesn't mention Janelle. They took her to a different room, and I'm alone, sky blue curtains separating me from all the action. "What about my friend?" I ask. "The one who was driving?"

He doesn't say anything, and my pulse races. In any other circumstance, I'd be proud of myself for talking so much to someone new. But not when Janelle could be seriously hurt. "Please, you have to tell me. Is she okay?"

"Who can we call for you?"

"What?"

"A parent, guardian?"

Oh. Right. If I tell them Mom's here, incapacitated, they'll call Dad, won't they? I furrow my brow, thinking quickly. I can't see him, not now, not like this.

"I just called my aunt." The lie comes out of nowhere. I don't have an aunt – Mom's an only child, just like me. "She's on her way."

"Okay, well, we'd like to speak with her before your discharge."

I grumble internally. Arguing with a stranger will never be on my to-do list, but what choice do I have? "You already treated me. Right? So, can't I just go?"

"You're at the age of medical consent, yes. But we'd still like to communicate with an adult regarding your care, if possible."

"Oh. Uh, she'll be here soon. But while we wait, can you please tell me how Janelle is?"

He keeps his focus on a clipboard. He says he'll go find out and to "sit tight" whatever that means. But he never comes back. A nurse walks in and changes some information on a dry-erase board on the wall. The tang of the marker fills my nose, nauseating me. Or maybe it's all these strangers I'm dealing with that's making me queasy. "Do you know what happened to my friend, Janelle?" I ask.

"I don't, sweetie," she says, swapping out the clipboard. She looks genuinely apologetic. "Just hang tight and I'll see if I can find out." Do they give these people a script or something? How much longer will it be before I learn anything?

I gingerly touch my face with my hands, assessing the damage. I can't stay here. They'll soon catch on that no aunt is coming. And then what? Will they call my dad? They won't have his name unless I give it to them. What about child services? Will I be taken away to be with strangers? A bitter taste floods my mouth at the thought. My heart aches to find both Mom and Janelle. To check on them, see if they're okay.

My clothes are rumpled with dried blood, but I don't care. I can only hope I won't draw too much attention. I go down a hallway of curtains that likely conceal other patients. I push through an exit door to the ER waiting room. People crowd the plastic chairs. An air of misery hangs heavy, so thick you can practically taste the suffering, tart and sour, like vinegar. I backtrack, seeing as the waiting room leads outside. No one I care about is out there.

I wander more hallways until I reach what appears to be a more intensive section of the ER. The curtains are replaced by solid doors and clear windows, and creepy, electronic beeping sounds pierce my eardrums. A nurse walks briskly down the hall, slowing as she notices me. My heart races, and muffled pounding fills my ears.

"Are you okay?" she asks, looking around. She seems hassled, like I'm distracting her on purpose. "Are you supposed to be back here?"

I clear my throat. Her eyes widen with impatience, and my words spill out in a rush. *"I'm-looking-for-my-friend.* We were in a crash together, but no one will tell me anything."

Her gaze flicks over me, assessing the state of my clothes and injuries. She must see that I've already been treated, hence the plasters, and she slowly nods. "What's the name of your friend?"

I tell her, and she guides me to a room where a cluster of people stand outside the door, wearing mournful expressions. One of them looks familiar – it's that guy in Janelle's room with all the questions. Her rude, way-too-forward brother. So, this must be her family. I hang back a moment, observing. An old woman cries into a tissue, and a man I assume is Janelle's dad hugs her. He's handsome for an old guy, his dark sideburns streaked with gray. I don't want to bother them during this emotional moment, but concern gets the best of me. I have to find out if she's okay.

My feet won't move. My legs are tree trunks, sinking into the floor and putting out roots. Her brother looks up. We inadvertently make eye contact. Oh God, he's caught me staring at them. I want to run back down the hall, run toward home, but I'm stuck to this spot, eyes locked with Janelle's kin.

"Hey, Kit," he says, and my face flames with the acknowledgement. He knows my name, but I never got his. I remember everything he knew about me, his nosiness, and his offer to help. He tucks his chin but doesn't break the stare. "You alright?"

How can I answer that? I fumble for words, attracting the attention of the rest of the group. If they truly are Janelle's family, they are much more wholesome looking than I expected. It never really occurred to me that she existed outside of my computer screen, really, let alone have a family. How dumb is that? The dad-figure tilts his head curiously. "Do you need something?" he asks with a slight Spanish accent.

I scratch my calf with the heel of my shoe. I bite my lip. "Um..."

"Are you Janelle's friend?" a woman asks. She looks like she could be her mom. Her cheek dimples in the same spot where Janelle has a piercing. "The one in the car with her?"

I nod.

"Oh, my word." She blows her nose into a tissue. "Are you okay? Did the doctor check you over?"

"Yes, I'm fine. How's Janelle? They wouldn't tell me anything."

They give each other silent glances. Red flag. My heartbeat slugs heavily in my chest.

"You know what," I say, suddenly chicken. "Never mind. I have to go. Just...I'm sorry. Okay?"

My feet are working again – finally – and I go back down the hallway. *Oh God*, is all I can think. *Oh God. Janelle.*

I hate this. I hate that we're here, that I'm causing so much pain, that Mom is struggling, and everything keeps getting worse. My vision tunnels, blackening around the edges of my sight as I stumble forward in search of a bathroom. Mercifully there's one up ahead, and I shove the door open, praying it's empty. No one needs to see me panicking like this.

Locking myself in a stall, I lean my back against the door, not caring about potential germs or plague or death spreading on my clothes. I cover my eyes and focus on the coolness of the metal permeating my shirt. My breath quickens. I count, slowly, to calm myself, but it doesn't work. I sink to the floor, shoulder blades aching from pressing on the door, knees tucked up under my chin. Imagine if I faint, and someone found my unconscious body. What would they think? What would they do? Probably drag me back to the doctor to start this cycle all over again.

I don't know how long I'm in here, but it's a while before my vision returns to normal and my breathing slows. When my heart settles, I tip my head back, gently tapping my skull against the door in frustration.

I have to face my fears and get back out there. The whole reason we're in this mess is so I could see Mom, and that's exactly what I intend to do.

Standing on shaky legs, I leave the stall and wash my hands with the generic pink soap next to the sink. I grab a second, third, and fourth sheet of nubby brown paper. Crumpling the towels between my hands is oddly soothing, so I indulge in the drying process longer than necessary.

I take a deep breath and dissociate for a moment.

I can do this.

Leaving the bathroom, I go looking for Mom. After a quick stop by the information desk where I study a map of the building, I take the elevator to the intensive care unit. I've lucked out – no one's manning the security desk to her floor. Maybe they're changing shifts or slipped out for a quick bathroom break. I don't question my good fortune as I pass by the desk unchecked. I read the surnames written in dry-erase marker outside each room until I'm standing in front of her door. Wires stretch across her massive form, and every beep of the equipment is like a mini bomb going off in my head. But her sleeping face is soft and angelic. No, don't think of her as an angel, because they aren't of this world, are they? I need her here, earthbound with me.

I stay with her for hours, watching her sleeping form, as nurses and doctors come in and out of the room checking machines, taking notes, and nodding at me with grim smiles.

I'm searching for the cafeteria, in need of some sustenance, when pounding footsteps come up behind me, setting off my panic mode. I've been discovered wandering where I'm not supposed to. It's the creature from the shadows, desperate enough to taste my flesh it's come out in the light.

I dart to the right, down another corridor, and stop before a bank of elevators. I frantically push the button, a million jabs in half a second, but of course that doesn't work, and the elevator takes its sweet time coming down. I abandon it and turn toward the stairwell, but Janelle's brother stands directly behind me, blocking my way.

"Excuse me," I say, staring at the floor. I won't meet his eyes again. I can't.

"Hey," he says. "Seriously. Are you okay? You came to check on Janelle but left without a report. It's alright, we can talk."

"No, I have to go." I move to slip around him, but he gently reaches out to stop me. Needles of sweat prick beneath my sweatshirt at the unfamiliar touch. "Please let me go."

He drops his arm. "I'm not keeping you prisoner here. I just thought you'd want to know."

I sniffle.

"I'm Toby, by the way. I realize we never introduced ourselves properly." A corner of his lip curls into a half-smile, so like Janelle's signature smirk I can't help but feel a twinge of longing.

"Oh." That's all I can say. And then, "She's dead, isn't she?" The words fall out of my mouth without warning, and I'm horrified but also partly relieved to get it over with. He looks taken aback by my bluntness, and I don't blame him. He wanted to talk, well, now here's his chance.

I wait.

He shakes his head. "No, she's alive. But she's in a coma."

I fight the urge to slink to the floor. She's alive, that's the important thing. But a coma? "Will she wake up? Will she have amnesia?" The questions flow out of me like water from a burst pipe.

He holds up his hands. "Look, why don't you come back with me, meet the family. We can talk about it more. They want to meet you, I'm sure. I just wish it was under better circumstances."

Yeah. Me too. I follow him back down the hallway, legs shaky and numb, terrified of what I'll see.

His mom comes up to me and takes my hand. Her skin is baby soft, nails neatly manicured. My bitten-off nails and ragged cuticles contrast miserably in her beautiful grip.

"Sorry I ran off," I say.

"It's okay," she tells me. "I'm Mrs. Martinez."

She introduces the dad and four other brothers whose names don't stick. I'm overwhelmed. I can't recall the last time I met new people and had proper introductions. Middle school orientation, maybe? I lift my hand in greeting like an awkward robot. "Hi. I'm Katherine. Kit."

"It's nice to meet you, Kit," Mrs. Martinez says. She sounds genuine and warm, if not sad, which is understandable given the circumstances. "Janelle told me she was staying with you last night."

Her dad asks, "How're you holding up, kid?" His eyes take note of the bloodstains on my clothes before looking away. It might all be too much. Maybe it's not fair that I'm conscious and walking around, while his daughter's tethered to machines, unable to wake. "You want to go see her?"

Do I? What will she look like? Herself? Or a messed up Franken-version? "It's okay," her mom says. "You can go in. We'll give you a minute. You want me to go with you?"

I hesitate, about to say yes, but then decide I'll brave it alone. I'm not some little kid that needs adult supervision. In my world, I take *care* of adults. "It's okay," I whisper. "Thanks. I'll go."

CHAPTER 16

I FACE the door to Janelle's room. She'd want me to visit, I think, just like Mom. Straightening my spine, I roll my shoulders back and hold my breath for good luck as I step into the room. The light in here is dim compared to the hallway, and it takes a second for my eyes to adjust. Janelle lies on a bed, a thin blue blanket covering her legs. Her face is swollen and bruised, probably where she slammed it against the windshield. Her car was too old – the airbags must've been faulty. When she wakes up – not if, never *if* – she might blame herself for not getting a newer vehicle, for not getting it checked properly, or for hitting whatever phantom thing we slammed into, but I won't let her.

She's hooked up to a machine that makes a steady beeping sound. Her heartbeat. She's alive. I'm so overwhelmed by this thought that I burst into unexpected tears. Sniffling and wiping my face with my hands, I approach her bedside with caution. I don't want to bump or jostle her IVs by accident. Despite the wounds, she looks peaceful, like she's napping.

Loneliness envelopes me like a heavy winter blanket.

"Hey there," I whisper, my voice too loud in this hushed little room. My face warms. Can her family hear me through the door? But she's here because of me, the least I can do is talk to her. I drop my voice even lower, a volume that I hope only dogs could pick up. "How're you doing? I hope you're okay in there. Heh. That sounded dumb, sorry. I don't really know what to say except...we're alive. I don't know if that's any consolation, but there it is. I met your fam today. They're nice. I don't know if you ever meant for us to meet, so that was interesting."

Tentatively, I touch her hand. I'm surprised to find her skin is warm – I'm not sure why I expected her to feel cold as a corpse. I pull back. "Please wake up. Please. I need to have a conversation *with* you, not just at you."

I press my fingers into the inner corners of my eyes, stemming tears, and take a shuddery breath. "Everything's beyond crazy right now, and I didn't want you to judge, so I didn't say anything...but we're here because of me, I think." The cat pops into my mind, and I suppress a groan. "This is all my fault. I'm so, so sorry. I don't know why this is happening, and I'll never forgive myself for what it's done to you."

I want to tell her about my night-walking and the terrifying *thing* that chases me home, realizing it might be easier explaining it to someone that's not responding, who might not even be listening at all. "There's something I haven't told you. Something bad. I was going to tell, but I didn't want you to think I'm crazy. I don't even know if you can hear me."

"Doc says she probably can." A voice in the doorway makes me jump. Toby walks in and stands next to me. "And that we should talk as much as possible to try and comfort her, just in case."

My cheeks burn with embarrassment.

"I didn't mean to interrupt you," he says.

He closes the door slightly behind him. All the air's been sucked out of the room. My heart pounds, blood rushing to my head, and I sway from the rush. "What did you hear?" I ask, nervously twisting my fingers through my hair, twirling the strands into knotted, raggedy curls.

He ignores my question, looking down at Janelle, brow

scrunched. He strokes the back of her hand, avoiding the IV taped to her skin, and sighs. "She was always a pain in my butt," he says. "You know how it is. Sister always tagging along, nagging. Wanting to play. I don't think I ever paid her much attention. I wonder if she knows how bad I feel about that."

Should I drop it and hope he didn't hear anything? He continues. "She was just so annoying all the time. You know? Toby, do this. Toby, give me that. Toby, Toby, Toby." He shakes his head. "I thought, as a sibling, a brother, I was *supposed* to be irritated. I brushed her off all the time. Ignored her. Made her cry on purpose so she'd leave me alone. I guess at some point it worked." He sighs again. "We don't talk anymore. I just moved out, started college a couple months ago. That's why I was at the house when she was talking to you, I was picking up the last of my things. We're not close, not like when we were super little. I regret that. I regret everything. You hear me, sis?" He leans closer to her face. "I'm sorry for how I treated you. If you wake up, I'll let you punch me in the nose as my punishment." He smiles at me. "She'd love that."

I'm at a loss for words. I back up toward the door. I should leave. Now.

"You're in trouble," he says, catching me off guard.

I pause, hand behind me, mere inches from the door. I was almost out of here, I'd thought. But he noticed. Tendrils of panic curl around my chest, squeezing. He turns from the bed to face me. I gulp. "Huh?" I play dumb.

He levels me with a gaze. "I know we just met but, what are you on? What do you use? It's to help with your anxiety, isn't it? But you shouldn't self-medicate. You should let a professional handle your chem."

My mouth falls open. He means drugs? Do I give off that impression? "What? No! Never."

I should've said yes. That would be easier to explain than the truth. Too late now.

"It will only make it worse, you know. You shouldn't do that stuff."

"I don't use anything," I say firmly. My quick, panicked breathing undermines my words, making me look guilty. I will my lungs to expand, to release me from this oncoming attack. Not now, not in front of Janelle, sleeping or not.

"No offense, I just worry about my sister hanging with the wrong crowd, if you get me. I know you spend a lot of time with her – I've seen you on her chat a few times. She's had some issues, and our family's been doing all we can to keep her safe. From herself as well as others."

Really? I look at her face, eerily blank. Is he saying she's an addict? She always seemed so put together. I thought I knew everything about her. Then again, she probably thought the same thing about me. "I didn't know," I say, breathless. "Wow."

"Yeah. It was becoming a problem."

Is that why we crashed? Was she high? How would I have known? I've never seen anyone on drugs before...I never see anyone at all. Maybe her personality that I thought was so cool was chemically induced. I hate thinking that. She's my only friend, and the thought that maybe she only liked me because she was under the influence makes me feel like scum at the bottom of a trash can. No, I don't want to think of her this way. Our friendship was real. We connected. I know we did.

"Sorry if I'm coming off rude. Hope you understand."

"It's okay." I twist my fingers together behind my back.

"Look," he rubs behind his ear, looking nervous for once, "I don't care if we just met and you don't know me but if you need help, you can talk to me. Can I have your phone?"

"What?"

"Never mind." He dispenses a paper towel from the box above a sink. Using a pen from a nearby clipboard, he scribbles something on the napkin and hands it to me. "My number. Seriously. You're her closest friend. If she wakes up and something had happened to you...I will do anything in my power to help keep you safe, like I was supposed to do for her." His voice cracks a little, and so does my heart. My breathing slows, the panic attack never coming to fruition, and for that I'm grateful.

"That's nice of you, but really, I'm fine. I don't have that kind of problem."

He tilts his head, expression changing from confident to curious. "Then what kind of problem *do* you have?"

I bite my lip.

"There's something else, isn't there? You were telling her there's something bad. It's alright, you can trust me."

I should be upset by his prodding. It's rude. But I'm not. I'm just too tired. Or maybe it's Janelle's presence that softens the tension. Regardless, how do I know if I can really trust him? "It's not...actually, it doesn't matter." I step back until I feel the door behind me. "Just, please let me know if she gets better. Or, you know. Worse."

I cringe.

He opens his mouth to say something, probably to remind me he doesn't have my number, but I slip out of the room before he can speak.

CHAPTER 17

HOW EMBARRASSING WAS THAT? My face must be the color of raspberries as I wave goodbye to Janelle's family, still clustered in the hall. They wave back, saying "take care" to my retreating form.

Was Toby telling the truth about Janelle? Maybe he misunderstood her. I don't even know him. He could've been lying to get me to talk. I rub the back of my neck as I exit the hospital, cold air rippling my skin even as bright sunshine blinds me. Now I need to find my way home, alone. I wish Mom were with me. I wish Janelle was too. Tears bubble up inside me, spilling freely. Why can't the people in my life stay awake?

How do I get home? I have no idea where or how far from my neighborhood I am. At least I have my phone in my bag. My heart sinks when I learn I'm an hour's walk from home. There's a bus stop just down the sidewalk; it would be faster and more comfortable traveling that way. I hug myself for warmth as well as protection as I approach and examine the map inside the shelter. This is probably my best option. Walking will take too long and be too painful, and I'm not confident enough to get a Lyft. Thankfully I'm alone now, so I sit on the cold, metal bench and wait. The large, rumbling bus pulls up with a fume-y wheeze. My throat squeezes with anticipation – I'll have to speak to the driver and make sure this goes in the right direction.

Gulping a few deep breaths, tasting the metallic pollution of the vehicle's exhaust, I climb the rubbery steps on shaky legs into the bus. "Hello," I say to the driver. He's portly and red-faced, but his brown eyes are kind. My voice sounds small and childlike. I want to sink into the ground and dissolve, but that won't get me home. "Does this bus go by Eagle's Roost subdivision?"

"Closest stop's Westwood Center, that work for you?"

I shrug. He helps me with payment because I have no clue what I'm doing, and I feel like such an idiot. Only once the payment's sorted do I turn and look inside the bus. There are a handful of people scattered among the seats, and I duck my head, avoiding eye contact. Feeling lightheaded, I make my way to the first empty seat, close to the front. That way I don't have to look at anyone but the driver. I sit on my hands to keep them from trembling. The noise of the engine makes my ears ache. There are no seat belts here. What if we crash in this enormous metal contraption? Would that be worse than what I've already endured? How is nobody panicking about this?

I hold my breath with every lurch of the bus, shocked at how much the thing rocks back and forth. I fear it will tip over as we tightly round a corner, so I keep my eyes on the driver, choosing to believe we're safe in his competent hands.

He glances in the large rearview mirror, much larger than the one in Janelle's car. I can see myself reflected in it, as well as others. But I lock eyes with the driver. He smiles. I wish to God he'd put his eyes back on the road, so I smile back, in case that's all he's waiting for.

His mouth opens, spilling worms and maggots into his lap. I choke back a scream. His jaw unhinges as more squishy bugs fall out of his mouth, a continuous stream, and then there's movement in the corner of his eyes. A worm wriggles free of his eye socket. It's long body, the color of red clay soil, slides down the side of his nose, pausing to lift itself, as though sniffing the air. A maggot follows behind, pushing his eyeball to accommodate the thicker body, and then both of his eye sockets become waterfalls of insects.

I glance behind me to see if anyone else notices. The distinct lack of screams or acknowledgement creeps me out almost more than the horrific vision before me. This can't really be happening. But the maggots at home, they were real. Weren't they? I mean, I felt them as they fell on my head, as they squished beneath my feet. Or was that sensation made up by my paranoid brain? Mom never saw them. How am I to know what's real and what's my imagination? Has my anxiety truly broken all sense of reality? If that's the case, then how am I to know what's really after me in the dark? Maybe it's truly nothing but shadows.

I close my eyes and count to three before opening them, hoping the image in the rearview will be normal again.

The maggots continue squeezing out of his face.

The bus still moves, following the road as it should. How can he see? Is he even alive? What's going to happen to us? In a daze, I envision the worst accident possible, a collage of tangled metal, splinters of glass, and blood spraying in a perfect arc. My fingers twitch, my throat feels gravelly, and my heart's about to explode.

I stand up, squeezing the bar across the top of the seat in front of me. "Stop, stop!"

The driver, the patient man who helped me learn how to use his bus, says, "Next stop coming up. Fairfield." His face has gone back to normal. Did I truly imagine the whole gruesome scene? How is this possible?

"No, no, I have to get off now! Please!"

"Fairfield's just ahead."

I sit down, staring at his face in the mirror, watching to see if the grotesque image returns. It doesn't.

A few minutes later, we stop and I depart, grimacing as my feet smoosh a couple of wriggly worms on the floor.

Real. It was real.

I'm still miles from my destination. But walking is infinitely better than being trapped in whatever that moving nightmare was. I pull out my phone, thankful to have it, and, squinting at the screen in the too-bright sun, follow its directions home.

Getting home is a relief so enormous I collapse in gratitude on the floor, the way a raindrop plops into a puddle. Walking took forever, and I'm already sore from the accident. It's been hours – I can't believe how long it's been since we left my house. It feels like ages since I've been here. Comforting and familiar, my muscles soften as exhaustion takes over my body. I literally crawl on hands and knees to my bedroom and nudge the door closed behind me. My rug, plush beneath my fingers, makes for a comfy nest. I curl up in the fetal position right here on my floor. My eyelids are paperweights; nothing can keep them from sinking closed. All the worry, adrenaline, and panic sucked me dry of energy. There's nothing I can do to stop the pull of dreamland.

Life's paused. I drift, head over feet, tumbling like an astronaut in zero gravity, unworried. In this soft place, nothing can hurt me. All my worries and cares fall away from my mind, the way crumbs dislodge from a loaf of crusty French bread. A warm sensation, like a springtime breeze, tickles my arm. It's only for a moment, and then it's gone. It felt incredible, and my heart expands with desire to touch it again. Whatever it was has moved on, and I lazily turn my head to see where it went. But there's nothing to see. Only darkness. It's not scary, though. It feels like closing my eyes in a toasty, pleasant bath.

Except bathwater inevitably cools and you have to get out of the tub.

It's freezing cold and a strange smell fills my nose, making my sinuses tingle. It's like the hospital...but where hospital antiseptic is meant to prevent illness from spreading, this chemical is sour, like vinegar, as if masking something nasty.

I crack an eyelid, followed by the other.

Darkness. Panic grips my chest, squeezing tight. Pitch black, as if my eyes are still closed. I imagine my pupils are the size of dinner plates, stretched to capacity as they grasp for outlines in the dark to make sense of shape and form. Sitting up, I run my hands across the hard floor beneath me. It feels like icy concrete. I crawl tentatively forward, feeling around until I bump into a wall. I glide my hand upward, the grainy paint rough against my palm, and stand. I feel for something like a light switch, heart pounding, dizziness threatening my senses until, yes – there it is.

Flick.

I blink, eyes adjusting to fluorescent lights buzzing overhead.

It's a morgue. I've only seen them on TV, but I imagine they're pretty unmistakable. The small steel compartments that look benign but actually house refrigerated corpses. My throat clenches in a gag. I need to get out of here, and fast. Those metal doors are all that stand between me and what looks to be – I count fast – eight potential dead bodies. Even with the light on, I sense the darkness gathering in the corners, moving in to claim me. I stumble on trembling legs to the exit. The handle is one of those push bars, and I wiggle it to no avail. It's locked. Bracing for anything, I bang my fist on the door. My pounding isn't very loud – the door is thick and likely insulated, probably to keep the corpses fresh. I jiggle the handle again, making sure I really am stuck.

"Help! Is anyone there? I'm stuck! Let me out!"

The air thickens behind me, creeping low, like a snake slithering toward its prey. I smack the door with my open palm in frustration, but it does nothing to make me feel better.

I turn around, scanning the room for the presence. My legs prickle with static electricity. Has it finally cornered me?

I wonder if I could hide in one of those compartments. Would it know where I've gone? But I can't try that. If I saw a dead body, I'd probably throw up and faint. Then I'd be chow for whatever evil is taunting me.

The door opens with a loud click, and someone enters the room, pushing a gurney. On top is a human-shaped form wrapped in heavy plastic. My mouth dries out at the sight. A dead body. An involuntary dry heave alerts the morgue worker.

"Hey," he says. "You're not supposed to be here." His eyes widen in surprise, then narrow in suspicion. "How did you get in?"

I slide past him without responding, and the edge of the gurney presses against my body. I swallow before I can vomit, acid burning my throat. At last, I exit the room.

A short flight of creaky wooden stairs. My feet pound thunder on them, and, in my haste, I catch the top step wrong. I stumble backward, falling, my elbows and shins smacking the steps as I roll back to that horrible place. My chin knocks the ground, rattling my teeth, and pain explodes inside my mouth so bad I wonder if I've cracked a tooth. But there's no time to assess the damage – I gotta get out of here before the thing gets me. It slithers in my periphery, up the stairs and out the door ahead of me as if it knows I've tumbled, knows it has a head start. Couldn't the man feel it? Is he part of it somehow? I scramble up the stairs again, this time on my hands and knees like a child hurrying to get away from the monster hiding in the closet, only now I don't know where it is.

Cautiously, I walk down a short hallway with a richly padded carpet – it lurks in the corner of my eye, likely enjoying the fear it's caused. I can't feel my limbs, numb as they are with adrenaline. I want nothing more than to curl up in a ball and cry, but not only is the creature here for me, but that man might catch me and get me in trouble. I keep going.

The walls of this place are papered in floral print. A huge vase of lilies dusts the beige carpet with yellow pollen, the sweet, earthy scent clogging my nose as I rush by. I must be inside a funeral home. I never imagined there'd be a morgue in the basement. What does this mean? Why all the attention to death?

I reach a foyer with rose-colored sofas, and ahead there's the exit. Almost out. I push open the door and leap into the night.

CHAPTER 18

I RIFLE in the kitchen cabinet, examining my bottles of vitamins and energy pills. I rattle a few, taking note of how many are left. I need to order more – a lot more – because obviously I can never sleep again if I want to avoid this...whatever "this" is. I pop an energy capsule and swallow it with a glass of tap water. Gripping the edge of the sink, I hunch over, letting my curls hang in my face. I shake my head, hair tickling my cheeks and stuck in my eyelashes. I can't keep doing this. Something has got to change.

A theme is forming – death. Or at least, fear of death. A cemetery, a morgue, the pool in which I nearly drowned. The alleyway filled with addicts on their last legs of life. It all adds up, one way or another. If I can't figure out how this is happening, maybe I can figure out *why*. Maybe that's what I'm supposed to do. Perhaps that is the key to stopping it.

I scour the internet for information, searching for people who might have experienced this too. The closest I can get are some articles and forums about astral projection, but upon further reading, I realize that's not the same. My soul isn't flying all over town, my physical body is. I'm scared to type my specific question, scared that people will read my words and think I'm making shit up for fun. I know I shouldn't care what they think, but I do.

If only Janelle was here. I could use her feedback, pick her brain. She loves puzzling over true crime shows, so maybe this would be right up her alley.

If Janelle can't help, maybe someone close to her can.

I still have the paper towel with Toby's number on it buried deep in the pocket of my jeans in my hamper. I dig it out and stare at his unfamiliar scrawl. Am I really doing this? My brain screams not to trust him, that he's a stranger and could betray me in any number of ways. But he's the only one who even remotely knows about my issues, and I'm desperate. Plus, he's willing to help. He's said so, twice now. What other choice do I have? Keep suffering alone, or take a leap and trust someone new?

Gathering my nerves, I get my phone and type in Toby's unfamiliar number. I craft a message, typing and erasing until it's acceptable, asking him to come over.

Toby knocks on the door. I open it a crack, confirming that it's really him and *only* him. The afternoon sun frames him with a golden halo, giving him the appearance of an angel. I take that as a good sign. Beckoning with my hand, I pull the door open just enough to let him through. "What's going on?" He sounds concerned. "Your text was so vague. Are you okay?"

I look left and right, making sure nothing else is out there before closing and locking the door again. "Thanks for coming," I tell him. "Sorry for the trouble."

"That's okay. But I am worried. What can I do for you?"

I take a deep breath, smelling the lemon and pine solvent I cleaned the house with. I was embarrassed at the thought of someone else entering the home unprepared, so I did a quick but deep clean before his arrival. Thankfully, no faces appeared in the suds this time, but a few squished maggots lay buried in the bottom of the trashcan.

I take a second breath for strength. He'll either laugh or help me. Here goes nothing. "I need your assistance with a – a sleep study."

"Um – okay?" His lips purse and he nods toward the couch. "Mind if we sit?"

"You go ahead." I'm way too amped on nerves and caffeine. I rub my hands on my thighs, resisting the urge to snap my fingers. "I'm fine. You want some coffee? Let me make you some."

"No thanks, I'm good. I'd rather hear more. What's all this about sleep?"

I inhale and catch a whiff of his scent, whether aftershave, body wash, or deodorant, it's reminiscent of how my dad smelled on his way out the door for work. Woody and spicy. I can't tell if I'm comforted or triggered by the aroma. I shift in my seat. "It's gonna sound...weird. And I won't blame you if you say no."

He tilts his head again, like a puppy. "You have my attention."

"Well, you heard me talking to Janelle."

"Yeah..."

"You know I have a problem. And you said to call you if I needed anything."

He nods, encouraging me.

"Okay, well I might've figured some stuff out, and I need someone to bounce it off of."

He sighs heavily. "Kit, I need you to be totally and completely honest with me." He leans forward and looks me dead in the eye. "You can tell me...what have you taken?"

I expected this. But it doesn't stop my face from warming. Of course he would ask. Who wouldn't? I shake out my hands behind my back, wrists loose, as the caffeine has me agitated. He notices and makes a pitying face. "Is it coke? That's got you all wired?"

"No, I promise." I will my fingers to stop trembling. I sit on the couch, leaving an empty cushion between us, and slide my hands beneath my thighs. "I know how it looks. But it's just Red Bull and vitamins, I swear." I take a deep breath. "I need to stay awake."

He searches my face, probably looking for signs of a lie. "Why?

"Because every time I fall asleep, I wake up in a nightmare."

"So, you're having bad dreams. We can work through that."

"No, it's not like that. It's worse. It's not a dream. It's literally happening, in real life."

"I know sometimes dreams can *feel* like they're real, but you have to remember it's just your brain playing around."

He's not getting it. I sigh in frustration and run my shaky fingers through my hair. "Look," I try one more time. "Tonight, I fell asleep right here on the floor."

"You did?"

"And when I woke up – I was in a morgue. Like, have you ever been inside one of those before?"

"Can't say I have."

"It's not very nice. Actually, it's pretty awful."

"Well, I don't think the general public is meant to be there when they're alive. They're hardly doing tours, now." I can't bring myself to laugh as he bites the smirk from his lip. "Sorry," he says. "Poor taste."

"It's okay. You remind me of Janelle, actually. But it's more than the morgue. Before that, it was a cemetery and a spooky costume shop. But worst was underwater. I can't swim and couldn't breathe, and what if that happens again? What if I wake up somewhere worse and I can't get back?"

"Underwater you say?"

"A pool, yeah. At the community center, after hours. It's a miracle I made it out of there alive."

"Really." He rubs his jaw. "Okay, well. That sounds serious. Let's say this is true and I believe you. What exactly do you need from me? How can I help?"

I pause, mulling it over. "That's partly what I need help figuring out. I thought maybe two brains could tackle it better than one, especially with my fatigue."

"That's generally the case, yeah."

I look into his eyes – velvety brown, just like Janelle's. "You know," I say curiously, "you don't look like an older brother. I mean, you look young, like Janelle."

The smirk is back. "But I am." He leans back on the couch, crossing his ankle over a knee. "Full minute and a half."

"What?" My eyes widen. "You're twins?"

"Guilty as charged."

"But I thought you're in college?"

"Accelerated programs, baby." He playfully flexes a bicep. "The youngest freshman at the U in, like, twenty years. I make my parents proud."

"That's awesome." I've never met a twin in real life, and I have so many questions (like, can they read each other's minds?) that I'm momentarily distracted from my problems. Why didn't Janelle ever bring up having a twin? Is she so used to being surrounded by bros that a twin wouldn't be worth mentioning? But now isn't the time for these thoughts; we're getting off track. "Anyway, I guess you know that I struggle with, uh, going outside."

"I gathered, yes."

"But how? How did you know? Janelle said she never told anyone."

"Kit," he says softly. "Why don't you ask me what you really want."

Embarrassment almost stops me from speaking. Knowing what's waiting for me tonight pushes me forward anyway. "Maybe – could you stay over and watch me sleep to see how it happens? A witness might help me put the pieces together. I was going to ask Janelle before – well, just before."

"Are you sure it's not just nightmares?"

"I already told you, no." He's gonna need hard evidence if he's going to stick around. "Hang on a second." I go to my bedroom and return with my laptop. "Here," I say, throwing down the gauntlet. Or in this case, the video. I give it to him so he can have the full view on his lap.

"What's this?" he asks.

"Just watch."

He does. I speed up to the timestamp I've marked then sit back to watch his reaction. Any second now.

Nothing. No expression. He saw it, right?

"Well?" I prod. "What do you think?"

"I think it's a glitch. Clearly. That's the most logical explanation. Your camera crapped out."

"You've got to be kidding me." I take the laptop and reset the video. "Here," I hand it back to him. "Watch it again. Closely, this time."

He humors me. When it's done, he shrugs. "Sorry, my opinion's the same. Technology can't always be trusted."

My heart shrivels, and I want to cry. The one person who can help and he doesn't believe me. "There's only one solution, then."

"What's that?" he asks.

"You have to stay and watch it happen. In real time."

We stare at each other as the clock ticks away the seconds.

He seems to be choosing his words carefully as if I might flip out on him like the dangerous drug addict he thinks I am. "I'm not sure that's going to make a difference," he says slowly. "What you're suggesting isn't humanly possible, Kit. I'm sorry if that's not the response you're looking for, but if this is what you need, then I'm not sure I'm the person for you."

Tears prick the back of my eyes, stinging hot. I slump down on the armchair, all the fight in me gone. I cover my face. I don't want him to see me cry but my body has other plans – it's need for release is stronger than my will. "I don't know what to do. There's no one else I can ask for help."

He hesitates. It might be the word "help" that gives him pause. "Okay. I'll do it. If only to get you to see this isn't reality. It just can't be. You do understand?"

I humor him with a nod.

"When do you want to do this?" he asks.

I'm too amped to sleep right now, so the odds of it happening soon is slim. "Tonight?"

"Okay. I'll be here at ten?"

"Thanks."

"Are you going to be okay here until then?"

"Yeah." I hate lying. "I'm fine now. It's just tonight I'm worried about."

CHAPTER 19

IT'S five after ten and Toby's set up camp on my bedroom floor, with blankets, one pillow, and plenty of snacks. "Are you comfortable?" I ask. "I can get you another pillow."

"I don't want to be *too* comfortable," he says, opening a bag of potato chips. "If I fall asleep, then there's no point to this."

He's right, but I still feel bad. It would be less awkward in the living room but we decided for science's sake I should fall asleep where I usually do, and that's here in my bedroom. It's beyond weird having a boy in here – or anyone at all, really. It's been my sanctuary, my place of solitude for so long that the physical presence of another human is tangible and strange. The awkwardness is so thick I can almost taste it, like pudding skin stuck to the roof of my mouth. I've given him a couple spare blankets from the closet, the only ones we have, and they're kind of musty but he doesn't seem to notice. Or maybe he does and he's just being polite, acting like he doesn't mind. Great, something else I'm going to worry about now.

"I've got my tunes to keep me awake," he says, holding up his earbuds. "Couple movies too. I'll be good. Pretend I'm not even here." He props the pillow up against the wall and leans back on it, legs stretched out on top of the blankets. "I need to stay action-ready in case something happens, right?" He is right, but his tone suggests he's only playing around. Soon, though, he'll believe me.

Instead of my usual pajamas, I've opted for a pair of sweatpants and a T-shirt. I figure he doesn't need to see my Hello Kitty flannel number. I would die. I brush my teeth in the bathroom, mulling over how strange this is. I've obviously never had a sleepover, let alone a co-ed situation. I wonder what's going on in his head. I wonder if he's ever spent the night at a girl's house before. My neck flames at the thought, and I immediately scrub it from my mind the same way I scrub my teeth, fast and furious. Spitting the foamy toothpaste into the sink, I wipe my mouth on the towel before looking in the mirror. I'm an absolute mess. My hair hasn't seen a comb in days and dark circles have nestled beneath my eyes like I've been punched repeatedly in the face. My skin is sallow and peppered with cuts that may or may not leave scars. My lips are chapped from constantly biting them. My outside appearance accurately reflects how I feel on the inside. Ugh. What have I become? My resolve strengthens as I swipe my curls into a soft bun for sleeping. I nod at my reflection.

It's time.

Turns out falling asleep with a boy in my room isn't that easy. I'm wide awake, fully aware of his presence. I keep my eyes closed and slow my breath, counting inside my head to calm down. It doesn't work. "Sorry," I say. "I might just make some chamomile tea to relax. I'm so nervous. Do you want something?"

"Uh, maybe some coffee? Help me stay up?"

"Okay." I fling my covers off and shuffle to the kitchen wearing Mom's old slippers. I didn't want him seeing my gnarly feet, and I hope that, just once, by wearing some kind of foot covering I won't be barefoot when I wake. My soles can't take any more environmental abuse.

I heat a mug of water in the microwave and plunk an herbal

teabag in it, swirling it around until it's the color of straw. I pop a coffee pod into the machine and press the button, the warming aroma of the beans soon wrapping around me like a cozy blanket.

I miss Mom. I miss making her breakfast every morning. I miss her asking to see my schoolwork. I miss the sound of her talking back to the TV when she thinks I can't hear. I just miss her voice and her presence. I want her to be okay. I want her here with me.

What I really want is for things to go back to the way they were. Our routine was limiting, sure, but it was comfortable, and I knew what was expected. This recent chaos will surely land me right next to her in the intensive care unit.

I carry the mugs back to my room and hand Toby his coffee. "Thanks," he says, wrapping his large hand around it, seemingly unbothered by the hot ceramic.

"I have energy drinks too, if you want some of that later."

"Nah, thanks. This'll do."

I hover, avoiding my bed. "What are you watching?"

"Have you seen the newest Spiderman?"

I shake my head. "Not really my thing."

"Ah. Right. Well, it's pretty good. You should give it a chance."

I settle back down on my bed, cross-legged above the covers, clutching my tea to my chest for warmth. "I don't know why it's so hard for me to fall asleep now."

"Sorry," he pulls the earbuds out, "is my movie too loud?"

"No, not at all."

"Is the light from the screen bothering you?"

"Maybe a little." But it's not the light. It's just him.

"I'll turn it off. Music only. Dark screen."

I sip my tea, eyeing him over the rim. I set the mug down on the nightstand. "How's Janelle today?" I ask.

"Still the same. Stable. Which is to say, she hasn't turned for the worse. Mom says we should 'count that as a blessing.'"

I hum in agreement.

"You guys are close?" he asks.

"She's my best friend."

"That's nice."

Silence grows between us. He taps his thumb on the back of his phone, a soft thumping beat. I guess there's no curing the awkwardness, so I say, "Okay, I'm going to try and sleep now."

"Goodnight, Kit."

"Night, Toby."

I keep drifting, on the verge of sleep. In and out, back and forth between wakefulness and dreaming. Like waves. But when I realize how close I am to sleeping, a dart of excitement jolts me back to full consciousness. I keep glancing at Toby to make sure he's still up and hasn't passed out sitting upright against the wall. Every time I look at him, he looks up at me, and I clench my eyes shut as if I wasn't watching him. I'm sure he knows what I'm doing, though, which doesn't bode well for my pride.

This goes on for what must be hours.

Then it happens. Yes, I'm sure of it. I hear Toby's voice as if from far away.

"Holy shit."

In this place of sleep, this blissful in between, where all feels good, why can't I reach the source that feels the best? Why does it tease me like this? I want to know what it is. I want to see it. Maybe it's the key to helping my wakened self. If I find it, chase it, touch it, maybe I will learn how to always keep this warm and secure feeling. I lift my knee to run, but I'm floating as if in water, moving in slow motion. I don't even feel anxious about how slow I'm going, my heart and mind cocooned as they are in velvet wool. My tiptoes land on nothing as I drift forward in search of the toasty glow.

Fear numbs my chest as all my blood rushes to my limbs with adrenaline. I'm inside a house, but not my own. A bedroom. Crumpled on the floor, of course, because when have I ever woken up in a comfortable place or position? At least it's warm in here and there aren't any corpses lingering around. That I know of, anyway.

I sit up and survey my surroundings. It's dark, but streetlamps illuminate the windows, outlining the furniture with a soft, golden glow. A bed looms before me like a mountain, dripping with ruffles – the duvet is the epitome of all things girly and feminine. My palms go clammy. There's someone – or something – sinister on the bed, I can feel it, the malicious energy forming a massive lump beneath the cover. I need to get out of here without it noticing. The lump rises and falls, and if it were human I'd think they were just breathing, but I know better. There's something...*off* about it. It's not rhythmic. It's *writhing*, like an animal in pain.

I scoot backwards, slowly, and wince when the floor creaks in protest. The thing on the bed stills, and I hope to God it's not listening. I hold my breath. *One, two, three.* I slide backwards again, closer to the door, but sharp movement on the bed stops me. I imagine the beastly creature, the undulating, glistening shadow with a mouth for a head, turning toward me beneath the blanket like a sheet ghost, seeing straight through the cotton and polyester fibers into my very soul. I bite my tongue to keep from crying out. Can it hear my heartbeat? If so, I'm doomed.

A foghorn mixed with a guttural scream, an unholy sound, rushes into my head, the pressure mounting so tightly I'm certain my skull will explode. I press my hands against my ears to block it, to alleviate the pressure, but it's resonating *within* my head, somewhere deep inside my brain. There's nothing I can do to muffle the sound. I scream, competing with it, and fail, my voice lost in the void. I fall onto my back, helpless.

The blanket rises into the air. Higher and higher, looming over me, imposing, *impossible*. The blanket slips off the thing, revealing every grotesque inch of its horrifying glory.

It's the creature in the window, only intensified, larger than life and filling the room, growing by the second. Still no eyes that I can see, nothing to indicate a face. Just a lipless mouth ringed with teeth like tiny scalpels, making room for its prey, ready and able to swallow it whole.

To swallow me.

I'm frozen, watching it reveal itself coming into the light, while my mind screams *run*. But I can't. Ice stiffens my limbs, my arms and legs weighed down with solid water. So, this is how I die. Will it hurt? Will Mom know what happened to me? I cover my face and brace for the impact of the creature on my flesh, preparing to inhale its earthy, musty stench. I can only imagine how it will feel: slimy, cold perhaps, and spongey, like an earthworm on steroids. Then pain as those horrible teeth sink into my flesh.

I'll find out in a moment.

The moment never comes. I open my eyes and recoil. The dark gaping maw of the monster is mere inches from my face, and all I see is wet darkness before me. "No!" I scramble backwards, holding my breath against the stink of sour earth, flipping over onto all fours to scurry away like an animal. That soul-shivering groan fills my head again, and I brace against it with all my might. I can't succumb to it – I won't. With a scream of my own to muffle its blow, I push myself upright and run to the door, slipping on a tasseled accent rug and nearly toppling over. Thankfully, I maintain my balance. The bedroom door isn't locked and opens easily. It isn't difficult finding the front door and I'm torn between wanting to find the homeowner for some help and not wanting to come across any more trouble.

I don't look over my shoulder; I just power my legs as fast as I can. Maybe no one's home because I don't run into any other people. If the homeowners were here, wouldn't they have come at my scream? They might be on vacation or out partying or something. I can't tell if I'm disappointed or relieved, a confusing muddle of emotions I'm starting to familiarize.

The door is locked but the latch is easy to maneuver, and I fling it wide open, running out into the night.

CHAPTER 20

I RETURN, out of breath and with a cramp in my side, cuts on my feet from the debris littering the sidewalk. Toby's frantic. "Where were you?" he shouts, and I shush him, worried about the neighbors. "You weren't here! I looked everywhere and couldn't find you. What the hell? How did you *do* that?"

"Quiet, please." I grab a bottle of water from the kitchen before plopping on the sofa, exhausted.

"I can't believe that happened," Toby says, pacing my living room. "I just – it's not humanly possible." His wide eyes are red-rimmed and bloodshot with peppermint swirls. He rubs them and shakes his head, groaning.

I gulp my water and wipe my lips with the back of my hand. I'm still panting from the exertion. I shudder as I recall the sensation of being watched as I ran. That thing is still out there. "How long was I gone?"

He checks his phone. "About forty-five minutes. Where did you go?"

"Some house. I don't know."

"How'd you find your way back? Your phone's still here."

I shrug. "My feet just know where to go."

"Speaking of." He holds up the slippers. "This was all that was left of you when you blinked out. Is that normal?"

"Basically." I sigh, defeated, and take them from him. Our fingers brush, and his skin is colder than I would've thought.

"This is pure lunacy, you know that, right?"

"I know. Sorry."

"You didn't, uh, put something in my coffee, did you?"

He's accusing me of spiking his drink. With what, a hallucinogen? We're still on that? "I didn't! I swear. I don't even know what you would use for a reaction like that, let alone have it lying around the house."

He stops and seems to be assessing himself, patting his arms, his chest, his head. He lets out a breath. "Okay. Sorry. I mean, what am I supposed to do with this knowledge?"

According to him, I disappeared in a blink, just like the video showed. No buildup, no warning, one second I was there and the next, I wasn't. "I mean," he says again, "maybe you fizzled a little beforehand, like static electricity, but I'm not sure. I wouldn't trust my memory. Because the second you were gone, everything before then is a little hazy."

While I was gone, he searched the house for me, convinced that I somehow snuck out and hid just to mess with him. Then he paced my bedroom, waiting, wondering if I'd reappear the same way I left.

Now he walks back and forth in front of the TV while I stare at him, exhausted, fatigue taking over my body. I need coffee. Or an energy drink. At what point are illegal drugs acceptable in this circumstance? I guess I shouldn't ask Toby that question. I sigh, leaning back into the cushions, my heart rate finally slowing down. I'm aware of my sweat and filth and desperately want a shower.

"So, this happens when you fall asleep?" he asks. "Every time?"

"Pretty much. Lately, yeah."

"Damn."

I shrug, too tired for words. Usually once the terror is over I can sleep safely for the rest of the night. But it almost got me tonight. It's never been that close. Will sleeping ever be safe?

"You want something to eat? More coffee or anything?" I push myself up off the couch, but my legs wobble from the exertion of running, and I pitch forward, grabbing the coffee table to keep upright.

"Whoa," he says, coming forward and grabbing my arms. "Hey. No need for that. Maybe you should lay down."

"I need a shower." I can smell myself, and if my own scent offends me, then I can only imagine what he must be experiencing.

"Rest is more important. Here." He takes my arm and guides me to my room.

I shake my head. "No," I say. "No more sleep. It's getting worse. I can't do it." A yawn catches me off guard, and I'm furious with my body for betraying me like this. I'm so, so sleepy.

"You said it only happens once a night, right?"

"Usually. But it's getting closer now. I mean, it almost got me this time."

"What did?"

Oh, shit. I don't remember telling him about the creature. If I go into all of that now, he might think he's in over his head. I groan and pivot the conversation, hoping he'll accept my rambling misstep as sleep deprivation.

"What if it happens more often now? What if I start disappearing whenever I just close my eyes?"

Concern softens his expression. "I'm just worried about you."

"Why? You just met me."

"You're important to Janelle. By default, that makes you important to me."

He convinces me to rest on the condition that he brings me a cup of tea – regular, with caffeine, not herbal. While he's in the kitchen, I sit on my bed and mull over my options. There aren't many. I can't tell anyone else about this, obviously. No one will listen to me long enough to get to that point. If they don't automatically rule it as fake, then even with video evidence and a witness, I'd be locked up in a padded room before I can even say "I have proof!" That's how the world works. I watch the news. Act first, think later – that's what it means to be human these days.

Toby comes back with a mug and hands it to me. My smile of gratitude feels more like a grimace. "Do you want me to stick around?" he asks. "I can, if you want me to."

Honestly, I don't know what I want.

I press my lips together. The thought of him leaving me all alone makes my insides tighten with fear, an unusual response when ordinarily I'd prefer it that way. Why am I so comfortable with him? There's something about his demeanor that's comfortable and easy to be around. Is it his shared DNA with Janelle? I wouldn't hesitate asking her to stay. "Would you?" My voice sounds small and timid, but I can't help it.

"Of course." He looks down at my feet. They are dark, grimy, and bloodied up.

I blush. "It's fine," I say, pulling them back. "This happens all the time. I wake up with no shoes and run home barefoot."

"Don't you worry about infection?"

On top of everything else? It didn't occur to me. They do hurt, though, more than I'd care to admit.

"Let me help you clean up."

Under my directions, he gets the plastic bowl I use for Mom's baths and fills it with warm water and soap. He finds the tweezers in the bathroom and comes back with a first aid kit. "Let's wash you off first." He's gentle but it doesn't stop the wince when he cleans the soles of my feet. I hiss when he uses the tweezer to pluck gravel and God knows what else that's embedded in my skin. I can't play tough much longer. Tears well up in my eyes, blurring my vision.

"There," he says, dabbing ointment on the cuts and placing bandages on them. "Walking might feel uncomfortable for a while, but you're all patched up. Better?"

"Better." I nod. "Thanks."

"Anytime."

He settles back into his nest on the floor next to my bed. "Are you okay down there?" I ask. "I feel bad."

"Nah, I'm good. I can sleep anywhere, in any position. I once fell asleep in my hamper as a kid."

"Your hamper?"

He chuckles. "Game of hide-and-seek. Guess it took too long to find me, and I just conked out, waiting. Happened all the time. Just ask Janelle."

My smile melts away, and his eyes grow somber.

"She'll be okay, you know," he says. "Really. She's a fighter."

The guilt burns my insides like battery acid. "I'm really sorry." I whisper so quietly I'm not sure if he even heard me. But he must have, because his hand reaches up for mine, clasping my fingers on the mattress. His skin is warmer than before, his palm dry and firm. It feels strange, this deliberate touch, but not terrible.

"Hey," he says. "Don't blame yourself. You didn't cause that accident. No one did. That's why it's called an accident. So don't go apologizing for something you didn't do. Don't carry that burden. You hear?"

"Yes."

He jiggles my hand, hard, clutching my fingers so I can't pull free. "I mean it. Janelle would punch me in the nuts if she knew I let you apologize. It's just some bad shit that happened. That's life; we bear the scars and carry on. Okay?"

His words cut me deep. His eyes stare into mine, and I'm struck by the gold flecks reflecting in the lamplight. I didn't notice them before. I blink and look away. He clears his throat and settles beneath his blankets into his makeshift bed.

"Do you mind if we keep the light on?" I ask. "I'd rather not be in the dark right now."

"No problem." He does that Janelle-style smirk and winks. "Like I said, I can sleep anywhere, anytime, any way."

Lucky him.

CHAPTER 21

"WAKE UP, SLEEPYHEAD."

"Hmm?" I'm on my stomach, face smooshed into my pillow. I kept my eyes closed as I rested in darkness, thoughts swirling with mouths and maggots, but little did he know. I was never fully asleep. Squinting, I push onto my forearms. "What's wrong?"

Toby kneels by the bed, my phone buzzing in his hand.

I take it from him and answer the call. "Hello?"

"Kitty Kat?"

"Mom!" I sit fully upright, suddenly wide awake. "Mom, it's so good to hear you. How are you? What's going on?"

"Kitty, the doctor says I had surgery. Is that right?"

Confusion crashes over me like a tidal wave. Doesn't she know? Is it pain medication that's making her loopy and forgetful? I thought it was just for laughs on TV.

"If that's what the doctor said, then yes. You must've. How are you feeling?"

"Kit, I need you here. Can you come to me, sweetie? I know that's hard but..." Oh God, she's sniffling. Mom's crying because I'm not with her. Shit, how do I make this work? Last time I went to the hospital, absolute disaster happened.

But I can't leave her there, in that cold, stark place, all alone. I'll prepare better and take extra precautions.

"I'll be right there, Mom." My voice is firm, my decision final. I will be there for her, no matter what. Come hell or high water, I will see my mom. I look at Toby. "Can you take me to the hospital, please? I need to see my mom, and we should visit Janelle too."

"Sure thing."

After a quick shower, I approach the front door with caution. My feet are sore, but that's not what's stopping me. It's the panic in my brain, sending self-protective signals to my body. Telling me not to go. Toby lingers behind, not pushing but not letting me resist either. "We can do this," he says gently. "Just take another step."

I wheeze a shaky breath, like an elderly person. One step, that's all he's asking. I've done it before. And then I'll do another, and another. At the end of these steps, I'll find Mom.

He helps me into the passenger seat of his SUV, not quite as old as Janelle's car, but not brand new either. I close my eyes against the imagined sounds of gunfire and thunderous windstorms swirling in my mind, as if I can trap my worries and keep them from manifesting just by closing my lids.

"You like music?" he asks, the car rocking beneath his weight as he slides into the driver's side.

"What?"

"You know, tunes for the road. Like a distraction." He slaps his forehead. "Duh, what am I talking about? Of course you do. Everyone does."

"Then why did you ask?"

He puts the key in the ignition and turns it, the vehicle rumbling to life. Suddenly a man's voice booms from the speakers, explaining a theory of gravity or wormholes or whatever. Science speak. I cover my ears as a reflex – I wasn't expecting the baritone thrum of a professor's lecture. He lowers the volume, and I feel sheepish for covering my ears like a child.

"Sorry," he says. "I like audiobooks. Non-fiction, space in particular. You know, theories of life outside this galaxy?"

"Um, sure."

It's interesting watching someone's face turn red. His cheeks bloom from pastel pink to a nice ruddy tomato color. Is he embarrassed?

"We can put the radio on if you want."

"No, that's okay." I put up a hand to stop him from changing it. "I don't mind."

"Really? Okay. If you're sure."

With the volume at a reasonable level, it's actually kind of soothing. The guy's voice intones softly from the speakers, surrounding us with his droning lecture like a cushiony blanket. The drive isn't so bad this time. Somehow, it's not as jarring, and it takes me a while to put my finger on why.

"It's different with Janelle." I don't mean to say it out loud. I'm so used to being alone that I've never really needed to censor my train of thought.

He asks, "What's different?"

"Oh, um. The way you drive. It's smoother, I think." It's my turn to blush. I feel stupid for even saying it. "Never mind, that's dumb."

"She was always a shit driver." His chuckle fades into a quiet frown.

I bite my lip. Is that why we crashed? Because she's crap at driving? "So, she's never been safe on the road? Is that what you're telling me?"

"No, that's not what I mean. Not at all. Just that..." He takes his time thinking of an appropriate response. "She's more aggressive. About everything in life, not just on the road. A firecracker through and through. Know what I mean?"

I do. That's Janelle, one hundred percent.

We're quiet for the rest of the journey, and he offers to let me out by the entrance so he can find parking. "I'll meet you inside," he says. "If you want."

I'm going to see my mom, but I'll visit Janelle's room after.

"Okay."

The bright lights and the sharp smells reignite my anxiety, starting with a headache that makes my skull feel like crumpled paper, and I pull my hoodie up like a shield. I take a moment to ground myself before I can fully panic. The floor is solid, the walls sturdy. The ceiling provides shelter from the elements. Nothing is happening, except Mom's wish. I'm the only one that can grant it. I take deep breaths and make my way to Mom's room.

She's awake and looks better than the last time I saw her. Not one hundred percent yet, she still has a plastic tube in her nose, all manner of wires stuck to her, and her eyes look drowsy, but there's color in her cheeks again. Surely that's a good sign. I want to hug her, but I pause. Is she in pain? Will touching her make her worse? She spares me the decision by making it for me. "Come here." She lifts her arms halfway up for a hug. I don't squeeze too hard though, just in case.

"I was worried about you," I say.

"They cut me open."

"I know."

"I don't feel a thing."

I glance at the IV dripping liquid pain relief into her body. "That's 'cause you're on drugs. Strong ones, probably."

"I'm glad you made it, Kit Kat."

"Yeah."

"How did you get here?" Her eyes dart back and forth as if she can see a mathematical equation in front of her that will give her the answer. It's not just that I'm here but that I found a way to travel at all. Her brain slowly connects the dots. "This is really...you know..."

"A big deal, yeah." I stroke her hair like I sometimes do at home, and the simple rhythm soothes us both.

Mom's eyes drift closed. "So tired, so sleepy," she drones. "But I have to tell you something." She grips the sleeve of my hoodie, but the material slips through her weakened fingers like water. I cover her hand with mine to still the movement. Her eyes, half-closed with dreariness, suddenly snap wide open, and she stares at me while her pupils flex and shrink. It's so alien-like my heart stops for half a second.

"I understand now, Katherine. I know what you've been trying to say all along. I'm sorry I didn't get it before now. But I do, I really do, and I am so sorry for putting you through it."

What? "Mom, what are you talking about?"

"I saw it."

"What did you see?"

"I saw what's after you."

My stomach wobbles.

She continues. "It wants you so bad, honey, and I don't know why. I wish I could stop it, but I'm in no fit state like this, here, where I am..." She drifts off, and her eyelids droop again.

My heart speeds up, making me dizzy. "Mom? Mom, hang on, don't sleep yet. What do you mean? What are you telling me? Something's after me?"

Of course I know that, but having her say it creeps me out. How does she know?

"Yeah, I saw it. I saw it in a dream." A dream? Or was it real? Is she herself being tortured in her drug-induced sleepy state? I take deep breaths and gather my courage.

"Mom, it's going to be okay." Whether I'm lying to her or myself, I'm not sure. I just know that something has got to change. I need to find a way to stop this thing. It's one thing for this hellish creature to torture me in my sleep, but I will *not* let it mess with my mother. Hell no. I'm going to end this, once and for all.

I just need to figure out how.

I walk down the brightly lit hall toward Janelle's room to find Toby and members of his family huddled around her door. They each look as tired as I feel, with some holding paper cups of coffee. A passing nurse tells them to limit the number of visitors in the hall, reminding them of the special waiting room down the way. But they're stubborn, and I see where Janelle gets her hard-headedness from. They remain clustered on the stiff plastic chairs lining the hall, and it seems they've dragged more into the space to accommodate them. It must be nice having that kind of support.

Toby sees me approach. "Hey."

"Hi." I wave a little as his parents smile at me. "How is she?"

"No change," her dad says, and he sighs. Everyone seems to be avoiding my gaze. I feel so awkward – maybe I shouldn't be here. I beckon Toby, and he comes closer. "Can we talk? Private-ly?" I whisper.

His dad gives me a strange look but doesn't say anything. Does he think I'm trying to flirt with Toby? At a time like this? Embarrassment prickles my neck and jawline.

Toby nods, touching my elbow and guiding me away from the group.

We move down the hall, out of earshot, away from his family. "It's officially the worst it's ever been," I tell him. "Somehow, it's messing with my mom now. And in this state, there's no way she could fight it off."

"Fight what off? The blink? In here?"

"Uh, more like...the stress that comes with it." Again, I'm not mentioning the creature. "Not that she's physically left the building."

"Did she tell you this?"

"Yeah. I mean, she's all doped up from the meds, you know, with her surgery and all, but she said it. She *saw* it. I can't risk it being just a dream. What if it's torturing her in her sleep and she can't wake up?"

"What do you want me to do?"

I don't know what he *can* do. It just helps having someone to tell, someone who will believe me. "I wish I knew how to stop this. There's gotta be a way, right?"

He shrugs. "I don't know what to tell you."

I appreciate him for not running away at my crazy story and tell him as much. "But now I need solutions. It's time to make it stop. Once and for all."

"How? Haven't you already tried?"

"Kind of." Now that I think about it, all I did was avoid sleeping (to no avail) and run when the thing came for me. What have I actively done to fight back? The answer is nothing, and I'm furious with myself for not realizing that sooner. Before my family was put at risk.

It's time to get to the bottom of this and figure out a way to stop it. I need my sanity back. There's something we could try. Something that requires total bravery on my part.

"I have an idea."

CHAPTER 22

"YOU READY?" Toby asks.

No.

"Yeah."

We move through the cemetery gate, the iron hinges squeaking in protest – or, perhaps, a warning. I shift my backpack, redistributing the weight across my shoulders. Inside of it are bottles of water, flashlights, snacks, a first aid kit, and an extra blanket. Camping gear. Brand new. Likely bought at some point prior to Mom's mugging, a trip planned to get me out of the house. Well, it's serving its purpose now.

We sidle up to the rows of headstones. "Which way?" he asks.

"Aim for the center?"

The air smells of woodsmoke and rotting leaves as we make our way down the path. I scan the tree line for anything out of the ordinary – but what is ordinary? The flutter of papery leaves creates a constant, ASMR-like shushing sound, so that must be normal. An explosion of bats disrupts the air – startling, but also to be expected, I'm sure. Twigs snap in the distance, and I stop. Fear turns my mouth to sand. We're so exposed. So open. Will that jogger be back again for his late-night exercise? Will he recognize me?

The center of the cemetery features a small garden circling a fountain, now dry for the season, and three cast-iron benches around it.

"Set up here?" Toby asks. "We can sleep on the benches. Might be a little cold, though."

"It's fine." I'd rather be chilly on a bench than warm nestled between the graves.

We put our stuff down and unravel our sleeping bags. "Good thing we have extra blankets," he says, and I agree. He sets an LED lantern on the fountain's edge, and its sharp glow softens the darkness around us – a circle of protection against lingering shadows.

I'm doubting my idea now that we're here. I'm not sure this'll work. How am I supposed to sleep *outside*?

Panic engulfs me, hot and quick, and I remember to breathe – I wanted this. I want to see if a new environment would catch it off guard. I've been playing defense this whole time, and now I've got to mix it up. See what happens when I'm already outside the house. If I sleep someplace scary, will I wake up back home, safe and sound?

Toby wasn't entirely sure about it at first, probably thinking about how he'd be implicated if anything went wrong.

Now, he seems curious and impatient for me to fall asleep.

"Shall we sing a camp song?" he asks. "Help you relax. 'Kumbaya'?"

"I never went to camp."

"Right."

Awkward silence. I look at all the headstones beyond our garden of respite. "You believe in ghosts?" I ask.

"Not really." He shrugs. "Not enough proof of their existence. Why? Do you?"

I lift a shoulder, uncommitted. Hadn't really thought of it until lately when my house got weird. But this thing out there, it feels too solid to be a spirit, so I'm not sure where that puts my belief.

With a big sigh, I pat my sleeping bag and lay down. There's nothing for it. No sense waiting around. I close my eyes, listening to my surroundings, quieting my heart. *It's okay*, I think. *It's fine.*

This has to work.

And if it does, then what? I find a new place to sleep every night? That lends a new meaning to getting "tucked in." What good would that do for Mom?

I take deep breaths to slow my heart and calm my nerves. My survival instinct is triggered. There's something about this kind of vulnerability that makes it impossible to relax.

I grasp onto that feeling and dive deep into the adrenaline.

This is *for* survival. This *is* my instinct. Maybe the adrenaline will burn off and exhaustion will take over. Maybe I'll hyperventilate and pass out. That'd be quicker, for sure. I can't bring myself to look at Toby in this state, so I stare up at the sky, waiting for the calm before the storm.

I sure hope the storm is more like a gentle spring rain than a hurricane.

I wish I could remember this gentle place when I'm awake. Things would be easier if I can recall this peace and serenity. I know it won't last, but I still try. That breeze of euphoric sensation skims my body, curling around me for a moment, before drifting off in the distance. I propel myself after it, even at this lazy snail's pace, and continue chasing that intoxicating feeling of elation, wondering if, someday, I might actually catch it.

A gasp bursts from my mouth, waking me, as my chest burns. Hot air scorches my lungs with each breath. Thick, acrid smoke clings to my throat, and I dispel it with a hard cough.

Heat. I'm surrounded by heat.

It takes a fraction of a second to realize that sleeping outside didn't work. My bravery was for nothing. Disappointment crushes my spirit, but there's no time to wallow.

I'm in hell.

I pat myself instinctively, but it's not me that's on fire, it's my surroundings. I reach into my pocket for my phone but pull out nothing but fabric as usual.

I'm lying sideways in the backseat of a car, my knees bent and my bare feet resting on a plastic door handle. It sears my skin, and I yank my feet back with a squeal. My shoes are gone, and though I'm not surprised, this is one time when I wish my feet were protected. They're in bad shape. I don't know how long they were pressing on the door before I woke up, and it's obvious there will be red, painful blisters when this is all said and done. But I don't have time to ponder this development.

This car, whoever's it is, is aflame. Tears stream down my face but won't do anything to put out the fire. The source of the fire is unclear, but it hasn't reached the interior yet, thank God. Can I get out safely before it does?

I maneuver myself onto my knees and lick my fingers before touching the door handle. I jerk back with a hiss – it's too hot. But I don't see any other way out – the flames already curl up the glass window with malevolent flickers. The air has a thick, wavering quality to it and smells like a gas station. The thought of fire reaching the fuel tank makes me panic.

Stretching my sleeve over my hand, I pull the door handle. I'll have to jump through the flames to get free, but if I'm fast enough, maybe it won't hurt.

The door is stuck.

"No, no, no."

Speaking makes my throat scratch as the smoke thickens. My chest tightens from lack of oxygen.

This isn't happening, it's not real.

More tears fall from my stinging eyes as I frantically jiggle the handle, desperation masking any physical pain. What does a little pain matter if I'm about to die?

A bench row of seats separates me from the driver's seat. There's an empty booster seat buckled securely in place.

I'm inside a minivan.

Apparently, a soccer mom totes her little athletes around in this van, judging from the vinyl stick figures smiling at me from the back window. Soccer balls, baseballs, and footballs are dotted all around them, illuminated by the fiery orange glow. A proud sports family. Where are they now? Why aren't they worried about their flaming vehicle? Maybe they've called 911. Maybe they're standing nearby, watching.

They'd have no reason to suspect someone was inside.

I have to break the window.

I glance around, desperate for something, anything I can use to bust out of here, to break free from the confining metal.

Gasping, my breath shallow, I feel around the seats and examine the floor. Maybe there's a soccer cleat or something else hard that I can use. I pat around beneath the seat and run my hand along the floor.

Aha.

My fingers wrap around something better. Something hard.

Wiggling it free from under the seat, I pull the wooden baseball bat up and test the weight. I've never held one before and didn't realize it's heavier at the top. It should work, though, right? I don't have time to think about it; I close my eyes and thrust the fat end against the window, hard. I bang it again and again. There's no room to swing, which is probably the best way to do it, but after a few tries and one long, drawn out groan from me, the window finally cracks like a hardboiled eggshell. Another few thrusts and it shatters. I whack the remaining shards of glass out of the frame.

The fire raises its voice, a mighty roar, and the flames lick the ceiling. I have to climb through. Bracing myself, I hurl my body headfirst through the window. My hands grip the steel edge to help push myself and they fry – like that time I accidentally touched a hot flat iron. But I can't stop or else I'll be stuck. I gotta keep moving.

The skin on my arms turns crispy with a sizzling pain against the broiling metal exterior. I dangle as my hips get stuck, and I'm forced to wiggle back and forth to get through.

Once my hips go, my legs slide out, and I crumple on the ground in a heap. I crawl as far away from the fire as I can.

The van is in a mostly abandoned parking lot. A flute-like whistle blows in the distance, and I notice the platform stretching long from either side of a squat brick building. I imagine it's usually filled with people waiting with tickets in hand.

A train station.

This family might've left their van on vacation. No one's around – as usual – to notice the danger right in front of me. My hair's singed, and my arms are bright red and wet looking. What degree burn is this?

I stand but the blisters on my feet are excruciating, and I collapse to the ground.

My brain swims.

What caused the fire? Was it natural causes, or did the creature make it happen?

I don't know how I'll get home from here. Trembling, I examine my hands. My palms are raw and look like fresh deli meat the way the skin's been peeled from my flesh. It stuck to the van, turned to ash already.

Sobs consume me – I don't bother fighting it.

This is it, isn't it? I'm beat this time. I can't run home. I can't even walk, the pain is so bad.

When the atmosphere changes, I accept it. How can I fight? The darkness closes in, and I almost welcome it; somehow, I know it will bring relief. Not just from the burns, but also the terror that plagues me day and night. I don't have to worry about it anymore. I can let it take me. It might be horrible for a moment, but afterwards I might *finally* be at peace.

The wet, slurping sound, like in that house before, meets my ears, but I'm not afraid this time. I want it to hurry up already. I just want to rest.

"Come on," I mutter. "What are you waiting for?"

It's funny that now I'm not scared of it, it takes forever to reach me.

The sound gets louder, but I can't tell which direction it's coming from. I don't even care. Just as long as it keeps getting closer, it'll be fine. It feels like it's all around me, surrounding me, just like the fire. I close my eyes and rest my head on the asphalt, registering the sharp bits of gravel and debris pressing into my wounds.

Just let it happen already.

"Kitty."

What now?

I open my eyes.

The van's an inferno, the black skeleton of its frame barely visible in the blaze. It can hardly be called a vehicle anymore.

An outline in the flames catches my attention. Am I hallucinating? I furrow my brow, trying to make sense of what I'm seeing. There's a person standing inside the fire.

Mom.

Is this what it's like near death?

"Kitty Kat," she says, her voice impossibly soft and yet so clear to my ringing ears. "You have to get up."

"Mom?"

There's no way she can hear me. My voice is too quiet.

"Get up," she says.

"I can't."

"Get up. You don't have time."

I close my eyes again. It's just my mind playing tricks on me. But another part of my brain scolds me for thinking that. That's what I thought about the maggots, but they were real enough. That's what I thought about the teleporting, but here I am. So why would this be a trick?

Her tone takes on an urgency that chills me to the core.

"Get up now. It's coming."

I groan.

Pressing my elbows into the ground, I leverage myself into a half-upright position.

That's when the form takes shape on the other side of the car, in the darkness. It rises, much like it did on that bed, only this time there isn't a comforter masking its grotesque figure. What once was shadow is now again a solid nightmare. Its skin, if you can even call it that, ripples and slides over sinewy muscle the color of squid ink, pulsing veins revealing themselves beneath. The mouth grows, revealing rows of needle-like teeth, so razor thin they're practically translucent. Wider and taller with each quick breath I take, the mouth drops open until I can't see the body anymore, until it towers over half the parking lot, up lit by the fire like a camper telling a ghost story.

I won't be able to get away from it. I can't. It's impossible.

"Katherine," Mom says. "Run!"

The desperation in her voice unlocks me from my stupor. What am I doing? If it gets me, if I die, Mom will be all alone. Who'll look after her then? A rotation of in-home nurses who only care about a paycheck? She's the reason I must live.

Pain rushes to the surface of my body, and I hadn't realized how I'd almost numbed myself by giving up. Now it'll be that much harder to get moving.

With every ounce of will, I force myself to stand on my blistered feet. With a broken sob, I take an experimental step, stumble, and pause to regain my balance, panting hard.

The shadow slithers toward me, its body undulating over the blacktop. Its groan reaches the very depth of my soul as its mouth drops open, hungry.

Goosebumps ripple down my spine despite the heat from the fire.

The van's gas tank ignites with an almighty boom, and it bursts into a bubble of fire. Hot shrapnel arcs through the air like confetti, scattering the ground, and some of it cuts through my raw skin.

The creature seems unaffected, still coming forward at an alarming pace. Why does the light of the fire not deter it when a simple streetlight holds it back? Is it something about the organic nature of the flames? Maybe it lives in hell, and its used to it. Is that where it wants to take me? I can't let it.

I take another step, and another, until I start some sort of limping rhythm.

I should be chow by now; I don't understand. It's caught up and lingers behind me, keeping pace with me like a loyal pet. None of this makes sense. If I hadn't run all those times before, if I had simply walked, taken my time, would it have slowed down with me? How was I to know?

What if it changes its mind?

Its shadow hovers over me all the way home.

CHAPTER 23

I COLLAPSE in my front yard and wait for Toby. How long will it take for him to realize I'm not coming back to the cemetery? I fade in and out of excruciating consciousness, until, at last, I hear Toby's panicked voice. I can't understand what he's saying – my ears are muffled from the roar of the fire. But I get the gist. He wants to take me to the hospital, and I agree. I should have gone straight from the parking lot, but the only way my feet know to go is home.

I lay gingerly in Toby's backseat. I don't bother with a seat belt this time. It hurts too much. This is a level of pain I never dreamed I'd experience, and I whimper.

"Just hold tight," he says. "I'll get you there as fast as I can."

That's the last thing I remember before everything goes dark.

———————

I've been in the hospital for two weeks now, according to the date written on the dry-erase board facing my bed. A nurse tells me I've been in a medically induced coma and had emergency surgery to treat my burns. My mind is foggy with pain medicine, so the details slipped in one ear and out the other.

I've been asleep since the fire. But what about the creature? Maybe the chemical sleep was so deep nothing could get me. Or maybe, as artificial as it was, it doesn't count as sleep. So many questions, and not a single answer.

I'm given my phone and I see dozens of messages, all from Toby.

I gave them your shoes and phone – left behind when you blinked.

They won't let me see you, not fam.

Hope you're ok. You got this.

I'll see what I can learn in the meantime. Just get better.

Words of encouragement, mostly, but also assurances that he'll keep looking into the weirdness taking over my life. I hope he's found something, because at this point, I'm stuck.

Dad walks into the room. He's shorter than I remember as a kid, and his brown hair's receding, showing an expanse of shiny forehead that doesn't align with my memories of him. But his jawline, square and defined, is the same, as well as his round green eyes, aged as they are by the unfamiliar webbing of crow's feet. His plaid button-down and khaki pants are slightly rumpled, as if he's been sleeping in them. My attention is drawn to his left ring finger, devoid of wedding band, and my bitterness rises like bile.

He pauses in the doorway, taking in my dressings. I catch the sadness on his face before he arranges it into a soft, unaffected expression.

"You're awake." He comes to the side of the bed. "Kit. How did this happen?"

I can only imagine how I must look – the white bandages wrapped around my limbs, my hands and feet bound with extra gauze.

I don't know what to say. I didn't want him to come, but I'm a minor, and Mom's still out of commission. I wish she was next to me instead.

"I don't know," I say. The pain medicine they have me on is

strong, and while it muffles my nerve endings, it makes my brain fluffy. I can't come up with a cover story. "It's all just gone wrong, I guess."

"I'd say."

"How did you know I was here?"

"They called me. I'm still your emergency contact, believe it or not."

What? Mom must have set that up without me realizing. I'm such an idiot. Curse Toby for giving them my phone. I'd never set a lock on it, having never needed to. If what Dad's saying is true, they probably had no trouble finding him in the system.

He looks around the room.

"They said your mother's surgery went well. All things considered."

Relief sweeps through me, and I close my eyes. That's good. That's so good. "Where is she?" If she's home now, who's taking care of her? I should call her. She's gotta be just as worried about me as I am for her.

"She's still here."

"Oh?" When I last saw her, she was improving. If it's been two whole weeks, then something's got to be wrong.

He continues. "It'll be some time before she's able to go home. And then she will need some help. I know you've been doing a lot for her, that's obvious, but I'm here to relieve you of that burden. It's not fair of her to put you in that situation. You're a child still and shouldn't be doing the parenting. I'm going to take you to my place until she's healed and ready to face up to her responsibilities as a mother."

"What? No, Dad. It's fine, really. I'm fine with it. Please."

"You can't go home to an empty house. It's not safe."

I want to laugh, but the seriousness of the situation weighs heavy on me like a ten-pound bag of flour.

"It's fine," I mumble.

"No, it's not!"

He runs his hands through his auburn hair, a touch darker than mine, and that's when I notice the graying streaks. He looks so much older now.

"It's not fine. None of this is okay, Kit. Look at you – covered in second and third-degree burns, and you won't even tell me why. You can talk to me. I know it's been some time, but I'm still your father. I love you."

I scoff, and he looks hurt.

"I don't know what she said to make you hate me," he says, "but I'm here for you, whether you want me to be or not."

"You left," I mumble.

"What was that?"

I look him square in the eye.

"You left us. Not just Mom, but me too. You didn't even call. Not even to see how I was doing."

His eyes glisten.

"I did, though," he says. "She never put me through. I begged."

"You could've called *my* phone."

"She had it turned off. Don't you remember?"

He's right. I'd forgotten. Once he left, we figured I had no need for the kiddie phone, and Mom cut the service. The phone itself is still sitting in my dresser, dead and lifeless. He never had my current number. How could I have forgotten? A gritty lump forms in my throat, and I swallow the uncomfortable feeling.

"I wanted to make sure the divorce wasn't negatively affecting you, but she blocked me. I'm sorry if you thought that was all me."

Why would she do that? Was she that angry with him that she felt he needed to disappear entirely?

"I have an apartment downtown. It's small, but I can make it comfortable for you. You can still access your schooling and everything from there."

I'll have to let Toby know. What would Dad do if he saw me

disappear? What would I do in this state – as injured, vulnerable prey? Will the universe give me a fighting chance? I barely made it this time. Will the circumstances change again, becoming even more dangerous? I hope not. I almost didn't make it. I was completely ready to give in to the creature.

But I can't argue.

———

Dad's apartment is small but decent. It doesn't have an amazing view or anything, but it gets plenty of natural sunlight. And it's close to restaurants and stuff. Apparently, he's living the bachelor high-life. Lots of takeout in the fridge, and not many fresh ingredients for home cooking. Not that I can cook for us anyway. I'm currently an invalid with instructions to rest and heal.

His place is a one bedroom, and though he demanded I take the bed, I insisted on the couch. I want to be out in the open, where I can see the windows, what's happening outside, even if the view is mostly of orange and brown leaves occasionally detaching from a single tree. It's something to look at. It's too easy to fall asleep in a bed.

I'm shored up with pillows on the dark leather couch, taking it all in and staving off a nap as best I can. I ignore the prescription pain pills and endure the stinging aches the best I can without it. I want to push myself to stay awake and see how long I can last. Sleeping is too risky. I've only pretended to take the medicine to get Dad off my back because they'll make me drowsy, and I can't chance it. It won't be nearly as strong as the stuff in the hospital – there's no way it'll fight off the blink.

Now's not the time to get lax, so I suffer the incessant throb of eight, still-healing skin grafts in favor of survival.

I've propped up my stinging, aching feet on a stack of pillows and spend some time channel surfing. My fingertips poke out from the bandages, and I jab at the remote the way a toddler would.

It's so humiliating.

I'm told I'll need to return for another round of skin grafts if I want to reduce the scarring, but that it won't ever go back to normal. I don't allow myself to think of that, to think of what my body looks like beneath the wrappings, because what good will it do dwelling on aesthetics when I'm in near-constant pain, fatigue, and fear for my life?

Dad's got every streaming network, so there's plenty to binge. He took the day off from work to keep me company but won't be able to stay tomorrow. I guess he leaves super early in the morning; I wonder, if I disappear, would he be gone by the time I crawl back in?

Dad's voice shakes me from my thoughts.

"Grub," he says, entering the room with a large box of pizza.

Toby walks in behind him, and I sit up a little straighter, wincing. I'd sent him a voice message updating him on my situation, and he asked if he could come over. I'm a little apprehensive about him seeing me this way, but I gave him Dad's address, thinking it might be easier to speak in person than over the phone.

"Hi," I say.

In the kitchen area, Dad's phone buzzes and he frowns at the screen. "I'll just take this, won't be a minute," he says, heading for his bedroom and closing the door.

"Hey," Toby says quietly. "Hope it's okay that I came by. I wanted to see you."

"Yeah, sure."

"How are you?"

"I'd say it looks worse than it feels, but that'd be a lie."

He grimaces. "Ouch. Sorry."

Dad comes out of the room, frustration etched in the furrow of his brow. "I gotta go into the office for a bit," he says. "Sorry about this, kiddo. I won't be long. Here, let me get you set up with some food first."

"It's fine," I tell him. "I got it."

"Really?" His face scrunches in consideration. Obviously, I don't "got it," but Toby can help me, and I'd rather Dad leaves us in peace so we can talk freely. "If you're sure. I'll be back before you know it."

Toby comes around the coffee table, taking in the sparse living room. It seems decorating was Mom's thing, because Dad's place is minimal, all clean lines and bare surfaces. No prints on the walls, no knickknacks, and barely even a throw pillow. He had to go to the store specifically to get the pillows for me to lie on. And food and drinks that I like too. He's gone out of his way to help me feel at home. But this will never be home. My place is with Mom.

As if reading my mind, Toby asks, "How's your mom doing?"

"Recovering. How's Janelle?"

He changes the subject.

"Are you nervous about tonight?" he asks.

I don't have to ask what he means. We already shared our theories about the coma medicine keeping me from blinking out. Which means here, away from the hospital, chances are good I'll disappear as usual. If I wake again, I'm too weak to defend myself.

I won't survive another outing.

"Very. What if it happens again and I'm still wounded? I'll be incapacitated."

He sits on the edge of the coffee table and frowns. "I'm worried for you," he says.

My cheeks warm stupidly.

"Thanks. I mean, you don't have to."

"Like hell I don't. Look at you. Does anyone else know about your, uh, situation? Your Dad know?"

I shake my head.

"But there's nothing you can do," I say. "Nothing's worked. You can't help me."

We fall quiet.

"Sorry," he says.

"It's not your fault."

I don't even know whose fault it is. What caused this to begin with anyway? Did I do something wrong? Something to piss off the universe? Why else would the mouth of hell pursue me like this?

"Well," he says. "Since I'm here, is there anything I can at least *try* doing for you?"

He eyes up my bandaged hands and feet. He doesn't cringe the way Dad does.

I shrug.

"Meds?" he asks. "Did they give you anything for the pain?"

"Yeah, but I'm not taking it."

"Really?"

"I can't fall asleep," is my simple response.

"What if...no. Never mind."

"What? What if what?"

He shakes his head, and I sit up a little straighter, which is only the difference of about an inch. He must have a theory. I knew it. Something clicked in his research while I was out at the hospital. Hope blooms in my chest as I ask him again.

"If you found something, please tell me."

"I haven't found anything, but..."

"But? But what?"

"I've been thinking. You're not going to like it."

Dragging it out like this is killing me. "Toby, come on. Just say it."

"What if...what if you leaned into it? Stopped fighting against sleep and embraced what's coming?"

I sink back into the pillows, deeper than before. The joy of hope evaporates as his words dry out my insides. Why would he say such a thing? Is he telling me to give up?

To *die*?

A thick lump in my throat makes me sound hoarse. "I thought we were friends now."

"We are." He leans forward, his expression earnest. "Kit, we are. Please, I don't mean it like the way you're thinking. It's only a thought. I just wondered if, by fighting it, you're missing out on the bigger picture."

"The bigger – what?" I scoff, incredulous. Am I hearing right?

"Maybe it's not as straightforward as sleeping and waking. Inside or outside. Living and dying. Maybe we need to think outside the box. What will actually happen if it catches you? We assume you'll be eaten. Then what? Maybe there's an outcome that our human brains can't comprehend yet. What if everything you want is on the other side of fear? We'll only know if we see the process through to the end."

"You're suggesting I sacrifice myself...for science?"

He shrugs.

I want to kick him out. I want to, but I don't. He's the only person I can share this burden with.

"It's just a thought," he says. "I told you, never mind." He furrows his brow but doesn't push the matter further. The small room feels even smaller with the claustrophobic silence that surrounds us.

"Hang out?" I ask, eyeing the orange glow of sunset in the window. Night will be here soon, and darkness. I could use a distraction to keep awake. "For a bit? We got pizza. And there are plenty of shows to watch – I'll even let you pick."

"Good deal."

He stays for a while, and we lose ourselves in old sitcoms, snorting at the shock of politically incorrect jokes and plotlines. I sense Toby watching me from the corner of his eye. Especially when I involuntarily whimper with pain every time I shift positions.

"Can I get you a drink?" he asks. "Or more food or anything at all?"

"Maybe a soda."

I hold the bottle steady with my nubs-for-hands and sip through a straw. Dad's being all eco-conscious these days, and the straws he buys are made of thick, cardboard-like paper that sticks to my lips.

I guess the colorful stripes on the straw are nontoxic too because the ink makes the drink taste a little funny. But I'm thirsty, and Toby seems pleased to have been useful, so I slurp half the contents of the bottle in one go.

A belch releases from my body, and I wish the couch would swallow me up like quicksand.

Toby chuckles.

"Better out," he assures me.

"Thanks."

He sits on the armchair next to the couch and crosses a foot over his knee, settling back.

"I doubt your dad would let me stay the night, huh?"

I'd be lying if I said the thought hadn't crossed my mind. I'm nervous about falling asleep on my own now, with no one actively waiting for me to get back. I want Toby with me to see it through.

"I wish you could," I admit. "I'm scared."

His brows knit together in concern.

"How about for now we just watch this show and try to forget about it for a while?"

I nod, and we turn back to the TV.

———

Something's wrong. The television blurs, and my head swims in heavy fog. Sleep rushes toward me at an alarming speed.

"Tobe –" I can't even say his name right.

My eyes cross, and my body rocks from side to side like I'm on a boat or something, riding waves.

That's when I realize I'm feeling less pain.

It's almost as if – but it can't be – I'd taken the pills. But I didn't, I wouldn't.

Did I?

Toby kneels next to the couch, propping his arm near my head. His face swims in my blurry vision.

"It'll be okay," he says. "It's better to test it now, while I'm here for you. Just trust me."

"Tobes...what?"

Before he can answer, the darkness swallows me whole.

CHAPTER 24

ALL PAIN LEAVES *my body as I enter the dream state, and I'm cradled once more in comfort. I weep tears of relief, not sadness. I don't remember what sadness is. That blissful breeze swooshes by in the distance, and my body arcs toward it in desire. I must have it. I move my arms, imitating the Olympic swimmers Mom and I always watch, propelling myself in its direction. I will reach it, I swear. As long as I'm here, I'll never stop trying.*

But waking comes too soon.

———

That bastard. He must've snuck the painkillers into my drink – it must've been the chemicals that made the soda taste weird, not the straw.

Fuck.

My stomach crumples with dread. My worries were correct – my hands and feet are still injured from the fire, and that puts me at a serious disadvantage. I fight back tears. Crying won't help me now.

I'm surrounded by hordes of people – healthy, vibrant, happy-looking people.

I stand, hunching my shoulders and grimacing from the weight on my feet. I blink in the brightness. Daylight?

No.

Floodlights swath the crowd in bright, clear light. That should deter the shadow for a while, I suppose, but why did I wake up here? I thought I was supposed to be easy prey. Unless it's hungry for a feast.

A cheer erupts all around me, people raising red plastic cups.

A bass guitar thrums the air, the volume on level one million. The marrow in my bones vibrate from the sound, and I nearly collapse from the sheer pressure of it. I've never heard anything at this decibel.

It's an outdoor concert.

The music starts.

Massive screens light up both sides of the stage so that people farther back can see the performance. The crowd cheers again. Someone whistles to my left, piercing what's left of my eardrum, as an older guy walks out on stage with a guitar and waves. His long gray hair is tied back in a ponytail, and his flannel shirt flaps in the chilly breeze. I don't recognize the music. It's an old band, the kind that my parents probably listened to. I have no idea who the singer is, and I don't care.

I want to leave.

People bump next to me on either side, nearly crushing me as they rush the stage. My body moves with the flow, like how I imagine being caught in ocean waves might feel. Claustrophobia strikes, and I quell a mounting panic attack even as my vision blackens around the edges. They're so close I can smell their salty sweat and musky deodorant. My stomach roils. I bend over, heaving, and acidic, syrupy Coke makes a comeback. I think of the pills dissolved in it, and fury strikes me once again. I spit and touch my mouth with the back of my gauzy hand.

A woman glances at my bandages quizzically, then smiles. Faux cat ears adorn her head, and sloppily drawn-on whiskers mark her pretty face. Her partner wears a flipped-up eye patch, a bright headscarf, and striped knee socks, a classic pirate. A quick look around proves most everyone to be in costume.

That's when I remember what day it is: Halloween.

Holy shit, I'd completely forgotten about this stupid holiday. The one where strangers come knocking, identities obscured by masks and hideous makeup, and even if my porch light is off, a few brazen jerks still ring the bell looking to mooch candy.

I must be hours away from home, because I'm unaware of any outdoor venue this size in my town. I see a clock on a bank sign, a giant advertisement, and it flashes eight forty-two pm and fifty-three degrees Fahrenheit and something about a "spooky savings plan!" So not only am I the farthest from home I've ever appeared, I've also lost a few hours of my day. That's new. What will Dad make of my absence?

How will I get home now?

Gritting my teeth, I force myself to walk normally, even though each step feels like millions of hot needles pricking the soles of my feet. I don't know how to get back to Dad's place. The only direction my feet know is to my house, so that's where I head.

I push against the mass of dancing bodies, moving in the opposite direction of the surging crowd. I cry openly as I do; no one can hear me over the music. A drumbeat picks up, pounding a headache into my brain, and the cheers blend in with the pumping music.

A vampire bares his fangs at me, then laughs.

The crowd presses in on me, keeping me stuck. My vision tunnels, my body giving up. But I have to try. Just one more time. Gritting my teeth, I ram shoulder-first into the mass of people, pushing hard and breaking through the revelers. My cries of anguish get swept away in the noise that's considered music.

Just as I think I've reached the end of the audience, another wave of bodies swells, blocking my way.

"No," I grunt. "Ugh, let me through!"

Popping sounds in the distance, barely audible at first.

Then, screams.

The screams rise to a crescendo, a domino effect, until all the happy, partying people collectively freak. Some drop to the ground, covering their ears. Others run, pushing and shoving, and I'm caught in the middle, tripping over limbs and suddenly unsure of what I'm doing or where I'm going.

I let the wave of people guide me toward the exit, the chaos surging behind me. The crowd propels me forward, sometimes lifting me so that I float, almost weightless. The lack of control sends a new form of terror washing through my body, clutching at my heart and dragging me down, down, down...

I stumble. Within seconds I'm trampled by the panicking runners. I scream, but no one can hear me over the din; no one cares. I'm stepped on, tripped over, and dragged. Agony, enormous, floods my nerve endings and blots out my brain.

The popping sounds grow louder – there's a shooter among us, picking us off one by one. We're getting closer, not farther away. The crowd shifts course, back toward the stage.

Is the creature using real-life people now to get me? Or is this merely a terrible coincidence? Either way, my heart rate's off the charts.

"I can't believe this!" someone shouts nearby. Screams turn to wails of anguish, and I know the number of injured is rising. I've seen this before. There will be video clips online within seconds, and I bet some are already livestreaming the horror.

Time runs out.

A quick, sizzling pain explodes near my right ear. My hearing goes fuzzy as a ringing sound burns inside my head. I bring my hand instinctively up to my ear. My gauze comes away soaked with fresh blood.

I've been shot.

The bullet must've grazed my ear, because it doesn't seem as if anything burrowed inside my skull. Small mercies.

Everything's in slow motion. I swim through the crowd, paddling the air with my gauzed hands. It's easier now, the panicking revelers parting like the Red Sea for me, though it's probably a fuzzy-brained illusion from all the confusion. No one questions my bandages or the bloody mess on my head – they think it's a costume.

There are people on the ground, some kneeling over the wounded, faces contorted in expressions of disbelief and despair. Some are laying alone, limbs askew, reminding me of the sleeping bodies in the alley except there's no way anyone's sleeping here.

I dissociate, blocking out the screaming in my brain, and let my feet take over with that curious pull.

I pass a group talking animatedly, as if the shooting is entertainment and not actually life-threatening. I stay quiet, alert for the creature that must be gathering in the corners of the darkness. My skin prickles with anticipation, and my wounds ache with a warning – it's watching me, following me. But I can't see it in this crowd. Speed is impossible. I'm blocked every which way.

Eventually I make it to the parking lot, an expanse of asphalt writhing with concertgoers seeking escape. Giant, brightly colored signs as tall as the lampposts display letters of the alphabet, designating a letter to each portion of the lot to help people remember where they parked and find their cars. I look up to see the letter "C" above me. To my left, "B" and my right, "A." I bet A is where I'll find the exit, and I'm grateful I won't be walking from "Z." My feet throb with the thought.

No time to wallow. I cut a straight path through the rows of parked cars. Some honk, a few tight blips, startling me, until I realize it's just the sound of locks being undone.

The hairs on my body raise. The goosebumps on my skin are not from the cold.

It's here.

Pulling every last shred of determination inside me, I dissociate further, detaching from the pain in my body, and run. It's hard at first, more like a stumbling speed walk, but my soul floats above me, watching – a complete out-of-body experience. It gets easier to move, because it doesn't really feel like me.

I run through the parking lot, to a windy road, to the three-lane highway whooshing with vehicles. Headlights flash and blind me. Police sirens pierce the air, and their signature red and blue lights whiz by in the direction I just came. I turn away from them and keep moving along the narrow shoulder. There are no sidewalks here, only dried out husks of knee-height grass and thick, decaying trees to my right. I stop and shudder every time a car passes, faster than the ones on my street, louder and more terrifying than that time I got the mail. I try not to think about how easy it would be for a semi-truck to clip me, breaking all my bones and leaving my body to rot in the dust. I don't think about what creatures lurk in the woods on the other side of me, hungry and licking their lips.

Sweat rolls down my face despite the plummeting temperature. I'm feverish with exertion and terror. Or maybe my wounds are infected. How long would it take for that? Hot tears well up and mingle with the cooling sweat. I can't go any faster. It hurts too much. Dropping to my knees, I bite my lip against the pain.

The shadow of the creature builds behind me, even as the invisible fishhook pull in my navel urges me forward. But my body won't comply. How can it? How can I keep going? This is the farthest I've ever been from home. Last time it took an hour.

Now it's a lifetime.

I should just let it take me. The idea, as horrible as it is, brings a sense of relief. To let go, stop running – what bliss. Maybe Toby was on to something. My body convulses with a ragged cry. Can I really let it end? If I let it swallow me, will it even be over? Or will I simply enter a new version of hell, a worse one from which there's no escape?

The thought propels me to my unsteady feet. I lean into the mysterious tug toward home, my face in a permanent wince.

I feel the creature watching the entire way, following, a gruesome shadow with all the time in the world.

———

Digging up the key as usual isn't going to happen. My hands are too blunt with gauze, now the color of an old period stain. But what choice do I have? I can't sit here on the stoop like a sitting target.

I kneel on the cold ground and work the earth the best I can, using my cupped nubs as shovels. The blood flakes off and mixes with the dirt, and the cottony material absorbs the moisture in the soil, weighing heavier with each damp scoop. It's slow going and barely makes a dent. I need to be faster. I need dexterity.

Using my teeth, I bite the dressing and peel it from my hand, gently unwinding it, slowing down as I get closer to my skin. I'm not supposed to do this, but I wasn't supposed to get the bandages wet either. I wasn't supposed to stretch and move my body, but it's too late now. Any healing that's occurred will have taken a giant step back. A whimper escapes my lips as the gauze lifts up to reveal the ruined skin of my palm and sticks to it, peeling away some of it from my flesh, despite the stitches meant to keep it in place. The cold breeze makes it sting even more, if that's possible. Holding back a sob, I use my newly freed fingers to unwrap the other hand. I hiss as it sticks and tug a little harder. The wound reopens, and blood runs crimson down my arms. This won't be good for it, but I press on, and quickly.

It's almost here.

I bite my lip, hard, as I dig, tentatively at first then becoming more frantic.

I just want this night to be over with.

The key rubs against my tender flesh and I yelp, partly with joy, but mostly from pain.

I unlock the door and turn the handle, pushing the door to go inside – but it doesn't budge.

What the...?

I wiggle the handle and try the key again, just to be sure. I bend close and hear the mechanism sliding into and out of place, open and closed. That's weird. I push the door again, but it remains steadfast. Ice fills my veins as I realize what this means, and I can't wrap my head around it.

The chain's locked on the inside. That means someone's inside the house.

My throat tightens.

I creep around the house, peering into windows, wishing for once that I'd thought to open the blinds and curtains so that *I* could see in. It's dark; there doesn't seem to be a single light on.

I hobble around the house and back to the front where I stare at the door in complete dismay.

Who locked it? Who got inside? Did someone find my key? Could it be the shadow creature? Or is the house itself physically rejecting me now? It always wanted me out. It tried frightening me with the oven door, by dropping maggots on my head, by giving my mother a heart attack.

By making me wake up outside without my permission.

Is this how it ends, then? I want to shout – to scream – to cry. But I can't do any of these things. It won't help.

"Kit."

I jump, startled, and whirl around.

Toby stands in the yard with his hands in his pockets, shivering a little in the breeze.

"You okay?" he asks. "Your head. Oh, shit."

He takes a tentative step closer but stops when I raise my hand.

I'm pissed. He drugged me. I wouldn't be in this predicament if it weren't for him. *That's not entirely true,* my brain whispers. *You would've fallen asleep eventually.* But more than anything, I'm frightened. There's no shelter from the thing now. We're sitting ducks.

"What are you doing here?" I ask.

"I thought you might be here. I came by earlier, but you weren't here yet. So, I drove around in case I could find you. You were gone for ages, nowhere to be found. I wanted to check if you came back. I was worried."

"Ha. Right."

"No, really. You disappeared and... I guess I thought it might not happen. You know, with your injuries and all. And with the pain meds, I just figured you'd be in too deep a sleep to...whatever this is. You didn't blink at the hospital, so I assumed..."

"You assumed you could make that decision for me. And bullshit. You knew I'd pass out. You assumed I would 'embrace it' and fucking die!"

He looks ashamed.

"There's no time for this," I say. "The house won't open, and that thing is coming." Even as I say it, something whispers that it isn't true. The hairs on my arms and back of my neck soften and lay flat. My skin, once goosepimply with sensation, smooths again. It feels like the creature's retreating. What's going on? That's never happened before. I look around, peering into the dark spots beyond the pools of streetlight. I can almost see it slithering away. Has Toby scared it?

"Kit, what happened? That blood's fresh."

I'm aware of how much worse I must look now.

I shake my head. He might be Janelle's twin, but he isn't her. He betrayed me. How can I trust him now?

"You did this to me. You put it in my soda, didn't you? That's trust-breaking 101, you know?"

"I'm sorry. I saw how much you were hurting, and I wanted to help. I just figured you were being stubborn and needed the relief, no matter the outcome. I am so, so sorry."

I can't argue with him. I don't have the energy. My shaky legs fold beneath me, and I sit on the porch, hard.

"Can you drive me back to Dad's?"

"No, hospital. You're bleeding."

I can't deny my body is falling apart. "Fine."

He helps me into his car, and I refuse to look at him the whole way. Instead, I ponder my options. There aren't many.

Why did I disappear? What happened to those missing hours

between five and eight? Why did I wake up surrounded by people, and why didn't the creature come?

Everything blurs, and I fear I might faint. Does fainting count as sleeping? Will it happen again if I do? The apparent rules are changing. The pattern's breaking, and there's no telling what's next.

CHAPTER 25

MY RIGHT EAR has lost a quarter-sized chunk of cartilage. The nurse tells Dad the damage appears consistent with a gunshot wound. His eyes grow wide, and he stares at me for a long time. There are live updates on the concert shooting all over the news, and the doctors and nurses give me curious looks, obviously piecing it together, but I don't talk. I don't want to give a statement. I can't explain it even if I wanted to. I didn't see anything useful anyway. It wouldn't help.

After they clean and redress my hands and feet, the doctor speaks to Dad privately. They stand just outside my door and obviously don't think I can hear them. The doctor is concerned about my mental health – the "sneaking out" and the wounds means he thinks I'm doing it to myself. Maybe for attention, or perhaps I'm suicidal. I think about how I almost gave up on the side of the road. How often I've thought about giving up lately. If I let the creature catch me, allow it to win, does that count as suicide?

"She may need observation at this point," he says.

They want to lock me up.

Would that help?

I stifle a snort by biting my tongue. Imagine. Locked away,

supervised, and still waking outside. They would all need meds after seeing that.

Part of me is tempted to do it, just for the witnesses. Maybe Toby and I aren't cut out for solving this on our own. Someone else might have tools to unlock the mystery that we don't. Maybe the more people that know, the more they could help. They say two brains are better than one, so what about several pooling their ideas and resources?

I imagine disappearing from a locked room and ending up stranded in the Grand Canyon somewhere. Or – recalling the absolute nightmare of the pool – thousands of feet under the sea. I picture my limbs tangled in seaweed and sharp coral, and the professionals up on dry land, scratching their heads as my lungs fill with water. I shudder. No, let's face it. I'll have to settle this on my own. I know that deep inside. I could have the entire US military behind me, and it would still be down to me and the maggoty-mouth-thing.

Dad is silent the entire ride back to his place. Once inside, he helps me to the nest of pillows and blankets on the couch. Only when I'm settled does he speak. "You left," he says. "You left and didn't say anything. You left your phone here, so I couldn't even call you. No note, nothing."

"Sorry." My voice is quiet and strained.

"That's it? Just 'sorry?' No explanation? Where did you go? That concert in Laytonville?" His eyes narrow. "*How* did you go? You left your crutches behind."

I'm so drained. I can't tell him; he won't believe me. I flashback to those conversations he had with Mom about my issues, and I know he won't understand.

"Can we talk about this later?" I ask.

Dad scoffs. "Sure, sure. Later's fine. There's no rush. No need to explain how you've burned yourself alive. Got your ear shot off. Right?"

"Dad. Please."

He stares at me with wonder. "I have no idea what's going on inside that mind of yours," he says quietly, almost to himself. "I don't know how to help you. But you can't wander off like that. I don't care what it's like at your mom's, we'll have different rules here."

I bristle. Is he trying to keep me away from her? Does he think I'm staying here, with him, for good? Not happening. This arrangement is just until Mom's well enough to go home. Then I'll be with her, the way it's supposed to be. How can he make rules for someone he barely even knows? Has he forgotten about my phobias? The very fact that he thinks I "wandered off" shows how little he knows me anymore. But I don't have the strength to argue.

"Okay," I say, only to get him off my case. I need to rest and prepare. My ravaged body won't take any more damage. If this last blink didn't kill me, the next one will.

It feels like a showdown is coming.

We don't speak. He just emits shallow sighs every now and then as if that's supposed to guilt me into opening up.

Fat chance.

We heat up leftover pizza, and I tense as the buzzer goes off. It's just the oven timer, different from the one at home, but harmless, and within minutes Dad sets a warm plate of pepperoni in my lap. "I can put it in a blender for you if that's easier." He points his chin at my wrapped-up hands. "Sip it through a straw. Pizza smoothie."

I don't laugh. Janelle and Toby probably hear all kinds of Dad Jokes at home and know how to respond. But I don't.

Dad smiles, but it doesn't quite reach his eyes. They're heavy with sadness. He maneuvers to the armchair and dozes while I stare mindlessly at the TV.

Something tickles my neck, and I shake my hair to relieve the itch.

A maggot falls onto my pizza, and I reflexively flip the plate over. The pizza drops to the floor, and the maggot wriggles in my lap, squirming into the crevice of my thighs.

I shriek, waking Dad.

"What's wrong?" he asks, dazed.

I jerk my body to fling the maggot away from me, and Dad leans forward, inspecting it.

"Is that," he says, "what I think it is?" He disposes of the thing, not as bothered as Mom would be if she had seen them.

It's happening again. It's happening here. This apartment is going to torture me and force me out. Why? Am I not meant to be anywhere?

I ask Dad to make some coffee. It's back to my nightly stimulants. I have to stay awake, because the next time I blink could be my last.

CHAPTER 26

OF COURSE that doesn't happen. It's physically impossible to go without sleep.

It's the same old shit.

Wake up, look around, and succumb to the dizzying agony of my anxiety before swallowing my fear and moving before the shadow arrives.

The lights are off, but a small nightlight provides a mild glow. I'm indoors. No crowds at least. An AC-like component casts a gentle blue glow across the floor. Dark masses sway in the cold, artificial wind. It smells like winter, and ice, and iron. I'm surrounded by hanging meat. The carcasses dangle from hooks.

A butcher's fridge.

The door's gonna be locked, isn't it? Every soap opera has a protagonist who gets locked in a walk-in freezer. I imagine my frozen body swaying with the racks of pork, beef, lamb, and whatever else has been slaughtered for human consumption. My throat constricts, and I grab the door handle. It's smooth against my fingertips and slick with cold. I push.

It opens. I breathe a sigh of relief.

A couple of security lights brighten the corners of a deli. Signs declaring their products are 100% pure and certified line the walls in bold retro colors of green and yellow, while a red ticket dispenser stands sentinel across the room next to the entrance. I hobble past a long, glass counter showcasing empty platters, the meat likely put away for the night. The tang of bleach mingled with coppery blood curls my nose hairs.

Has any of this been caught on camera? I imagine some of these places have CCTV equipment. Will someone eventually see me on the footage and wonder how I got there? Maybe I should just lie down and let them watch what happens. I'm so tired of running, of fighting.

Survival instinct is the only thing that keeps me going.

The lights flicker. The walls curl in on themselves, like four waves coming in for a hug on all sides. My legs sway as if in response, and that's my signal to leave. But it's not without difficulty. My body, rippling in sync with the walls, won't listen to my brain's instruction. I'm no longer in control of myself. My ribs tighten, breath wheezing from my lungs.

I won't have much time before it appears.

I shuffle toward the front of the business, agonizingly slow. Where is it? It should be lurking behind me now. It could swallow me faster than a blink, I'm such easy prey. I guess that was its intention all along – weaken me, slow me down. Well, it got me to stop running. I can barely move. So why hasn't it eaten me yet?

What will it feel like when it does?

I anticipate that slap of darkness and sting of teeth with each passing second. But it doesn't come. The energy still wavers all around me as I unlock the door and push it open.

I wish my feet knew the way to Dad's apartment. There's no point going back home. My front door's still locked. The key is useless.

Facing the street, I look up and down the road, waiting for the creature to show up. My muscles tighten, painfully stretching my skin, prepared to snap into motion at the first sign of it.

The atmosphere wavers in the distance, just like in the deli, signaling its arrival. Its energy changes the air, sucking and warping it. I hunch my shoulders in defense. The wind turns icy, hissing though my hair, leaving icicles in my strands. I swear there's a voice in it, quiet yet firm, and devoid of gender, curling inside my ear and slithering around my brain. Saying my name. Calling me from inside myself. My mouth waters as my body prepares to vomit, a futile attempt to purge the invading voice. It won't do any good, so I swallow the nausea and pull myself upright.

I stand my ground. This is home base, my turf.

Untouchable.

But a part of my mind whispers of all the horrible things going on inside the house, the things I believe the creature has caused. The face in the oven cleaner. The maggots. Shit, even the locked door. I'm suddenly not so sure, but I refuse to budge. If I run now, then that's it, there's nowhere else to go.

The wind changes direction. It moves backward, picking up speed, pulling me away from the house, toward *it*. And then...

Nothing.

The world goes silent, all noise sucked away like a vacuum, before rushing forward again like a hurricane.

I duck, squinting to protect my eyes from the leaves and debris that pick up in the wind.

Shielding my face, I look up through my fingers – and recoil.

The shadowy creature fills the street with its once again solid form, its monstrous, rippling body sliding in my direction at top speed. There's no time to process. It'll reach me in three...

two...

I run as fast as I can. So fast my feet don't touch the ground. I must be flying – I've sprouted wings that lift me into the air, that flap away the pain so that I can get away from this nightmare.

I have no destination in mind, just movement that carries me forward, blood filling my pumping limbs. Wounds? What wounds? Adrenaline masks all injury. I'm healthy again, well-rested and strong. I am faster than it. I'm –

I stumble, tripping over my own foot, and land hard on the ground. All sensation comes rushing back. The hopeful illusion is shattered. I'll never make it.

Something tells me this is my last chance.

The creature gains on me in these few precious seconds, seconds that I can't spare.

No, no, I have to get up. This is the last time I fall.

This is the last time I run.

With a groan that turns into a primal roar, I pitch forward as I feel the presence of the creature at my back. Haltingly, I move away, picking up pace again when I find my feet.

My arms pump furiously, my breath coming in short spurts. I can almost hear it crying out for me, like it wants me to wait. That's weird. It wouldn't do that.

It wants to eat me. Doesn't it?

Everything blurs. A cramp forms in my side, the first human consequence of choosing the latter of fight-or-flight.

I slow down, reluctant, but I can't keep going like this. I'm not fit enough. Injuries aside, yoga doesn't provide much in the way of cardio, and it shows. My heart doesn't know how to keep up with the increased demand for circulation. Will I have a heart attack like Mom?

Now that I've stopped, my senses awaken to my surroundings. The breeze picks up, and the air smells damp and briny, like sushi that's been left out too long. The mechanical hum of car engines gives way to the bubbling gurgle of water. I step forward toward a short stone wall at the side of the road and look over it.

My mouth dries, tongue instantly going fuzzy when I realize I'm on a bridge. The same one Mom jumped off that night so many years ago.

CHAPTER 27

I DIDN'T KNOW I was coming this way, didn't recognize the landscape. I clutch the waist-high stone barrier that prevents cars from going over the edge, the gritty texture sending electric pings through my wet and bloody hands. Panting hard, I stare at the water below as it rushes, high and excited by the rain we've had. What hairs I have left on my body stand at attention, prickling. I sense the creature creeping behind me, blocking me from escaping.

Time slows in what is now becoming a familiar underwater sensation when it's near. The creature exhales a foul odor of rotten meat, sulfuric and awful. The scent clings inside my nostrils. The breath, humid and warm, is a sharp contrast to the cold breeze blowing tonight.

It looms above, poised to consume me in one easy gulp. Its mouth opens long. Every nodule on its foul tongue pulsates and glistens with desire for a taste. Breath smelling of earth and rotten meat puffs directly over my head, and I gag.

I don't know how to fight. I throw a rock, but it barely makes a squelch as it hits my target. I'm sure punching the creature won't be much better, in fact, offering my arm might tempt it to bite. I'm trapped with no way out. There's nothing but pain and darkness coming for me, no hope of escape.

I shiver, queasy, before vomiting soured pizza all over my feet. Is this how it ends for me? I thought I was stronger. I thought I could survive this. That's why I called Toby, why I fought so hard to stay alive.

I think of Mom and how desperate she must've felt all those years ago, desperate enough to stand where I am now. To do what she did. Am I at that same level of desperation? I'm going to die either way, so wouldn't it be better if it's my choice, something I do myself, rather than letting this literal nightmare decide for me?

I lean over the damp stone and imagine what it might feel like to hit the water. I never asked Mom about it. Maybe that's for the best.

I'd have to aim just right and jump close to that bank of rocks, hoping I don't just break some bones, but hit my head or snap my neck.

I lift a knee to crawl up and over the wall as though in a dream. Nothing feels solid anymore. It's like I'm already gone.

Will anyone know what happened? Will there be evidence, some shred of proof, of how this went down? Or will Mom be left wondering why I ran away? Tears stream down my face unchecked. Will Dad go to her, console her? Will he also need comforting in the loss of his weird daughter, the neurotic little girl he barely knew?

I spare a thought for Janelle, my one true friend, and hope she'll understand. Maybe Toby will explain it to her.

Both legs over the barrier, I lean forward, hanging on by the tips of my tingly fingers. I just have to shift my weight an inch or two and then I'll fly for real.

I just have to let go.

I can do it.

Just do it.

A gargled sound bubbles up my throat, a cross between a shout, a sob, and laughter.

I can't do it. I'm not ready to die. That's why I've been running and fighting this. I guess I'm not at the point Mom was after all, which makes my heart squeeze for her. To be able to let go and plunge to the cold and pain and darkness below – she must've been experiencing a feeling I may never know, a feeling worse than death.

"I'm so sorry," I whisper.

Sobs choke my words.

I've got to turn around. I need to get on the other side of the wall. But my fingers are now frozen stiff, numb with tension, and I'm afraid if I move, I'll slip.

The creature seems to be waiting, like it senses its prey is about to become mashed potatoes and wouldn't mind a little creamy texture.

It makes that awful sound, the one that clamors inside my head, and my skull's going to implode. Something's gotta give. It's as if it's realized I'm not jumping and I'm still on the menu, in one piece. But I won't be, not today.

My fingers slip from the edge. I clench them, scrabbling for purchase on the stone, but no luck. My belly swoops as my body gives in to gravity and plunges to the icy river below. A shriek meets my ears, and I realize it's coming from me.

My body flips, feet over head, and I tense, preparing for the shattering impact.

And then –

The mouth opens wide above me, and the wet throat envelopes me in darkness.

It's done.

Captured before I hit the water.

I didn't get a chance to suck in a breath after my scream, and now I inhale a nose full of burning acid. I cough, desperate for air, but I can already feel the digestive enzymes working on my body, dissolving my skin both new and old and eating away at my flesh.

I'm inside the beast now, and it's terrible.

Then, suddenly, I'm not. My eyes open, not to darkness, but to find that my body, weightless, floats in a place both light and dark. There's no light source that I can determine, but I see as clearly as if it's broad daylight. My belly is warm and content, and somehow, I'm no longer afraid. Something about all this is very familiar. There's a connection here, wherever "here" is, between me and the space around me.

Am I dead? Is this heaven? It can't be hell – there are no flames or demons. In fact, I'm feeling very, very good. Like I'm tucked up in a safe, cozy cocoon of love and contentment.

Somehow, I know in my bones I can't stay. It's not knowledge in my head, an understanding that my mind can wrap around with a clean description. It simply *is*.

I'm not meant to be here yet.

This is just a glimpse.

But I don't want to leave. I want to stay here forever. This is the first time in years, in such a long time that feels like forever, that I'm relaxed. Content. Happy.

I hear Mom's voice in my head. "No, Kitty! Fight!"

Why would she say that? Doesn't she know it's better here? A good place? A safe place? I could stay here for eternity. It's a bliss I've never –

Wait.

Is this just a hallucination? Like a slow poison meant to paralyze prey for easier digestion? The thought fills me with a white-hot rage that burns away the comfort cocoon, and I'm left with sizzling pain all over my body, my flesh dissolving in the acidic goo. I'm turning to mush.

The rage turns to panic, and I can't think straight. What do I do? How do I get out of here? I think of my yogic breath work and meditation, how it always calmed me and helped me focus. I can't take deep breaths now, but I can visualize it.

I close my eyes and count, imagining my lungs filling with fresh, clean air.

One, two, three, hold. Release.

Repeat.

I'm outside of my head now, and my body knows what to do.

I'm sliding down an endless, undulating, tongue-like muscle, deeper into the beast. If I get too far down, I won't be able to climb back out. I kick and punch at the slimy wall of tissue, hoping it will spit me back out. I dig my fingers into the smooth, sinewy wall of what must be its throat, and press my feet into the opposite side to slow my descent. Hopefully it gives the sensation of something lodged in its gullet, like when you choke on a cough drop or swallow down the wrong pipe.

My nails scrape the meaty flesh. It's like raw chicken, and some of it collects beneath my nails in clumps.

Although it's dark and I can't see, I can tell I'm going further down into its belly.

The sides do a wave-like motion, closing in on me and releasing again, the same way the atmosphere changed as it drew near. They ripple again, from bottom to top, squeezing me and releasing. I press harder, ensuring I remain stationary.

A stench unlike anything I've ever smelled engulfs me. I gag, my arms weakening, and I slip down a little more. Liquid surges upward, sloshing over my feet and soaking my clothes with what must be bile. I thought it burned in here before, but the acid tsunami truly brings the sting as my skin dissolves.

The thing must be gagging, about to throw up, hopefully purging me with it.

I keep scraping.

Like a busted fire hydrant, a powerful surge rises beneath me, pushing me upward. I see light from beyond the rows of microscopic teeth. I ride the wave, and those teeth scrape my tender flesh until I plop unceremoniously onto the ground in a large pool of rank fluid. I cough the burning substance out of my lungs, trading it for fresh air.

I'm not on the bridge anymore. I'm on the riverbank, half-covered in sand. My feet are submerged in the cool water as the murky, fishy waves lap at my calves with the chill of frozen razor blades.

The shadow drapes over me like a blanket. It unfurls itself, slowly, excruciatingly, until its long body hovers above me. Something's different this time. Its eyes, usually impossible to see, now bore into mine as intense little black dots, as if sizing me up. Did I puzzle it?

A cracking sound pierces the air. Something protrudes from its side that wasn't there before. It looks like a bone, a rib bone, slicing through the gelatinous mass. Does it even have a skeleton? Another loud crack, and a second narrow protrusion bursts through, the tip pointy like a sharpened spear. Another, and another, faster and faster. A whole ribcage snapping, one long ripping noise as what seems like hundreds of these things poke out of it, flanking either side like the legs of a centipede. What are those? Why is it doing this now?

"Kitty!" My name is called from a distance.

Is that Mom's voice? It can't be. No way. But there she is, on the other side of the river, running toward me.

Running.

It can't be her. First of all, she can barely walk, let alone run. This version of Mom is hundreds of pounds lighter. She's wearing a long, flowy pink dress that shows off her lean figure. She looks just like she did when I was little.

"Kitty!" she shouts.

Another voice meets me from the other direction.

"Kit."

Toby? How did he find me here?

"Kit, it's okay," he says. "You're going to be okay. Everything is fine."

"Kitty," Mom cries, her dress flapping around her legs. "You have to listen to me. Listen to me!"

What is this? What's going on?

"Mom?" My throat burns raw. "How did you get here?"

"There's no time. You have to do this. Now!"

"Do what?" She's not making sense.

Toby reaches down and clasps my arms in his warm, dry hands, helping me to my feet. "There you go," he says. He doesn't acknowledge my mother screaming from the other side of the river. Can he not see her? Is this a hallucination, a byproduct of the creature's dark magic?

"Toby," I rasp. "Do you see her?"

His brows knit together. He sweeps his gaze along the river before landing on me.

"See who?"

Mom waves her arms above her head, frantic. What's the deal? He can't miss her. "My mom. She's right over there. She's...different."

I still can't get over how she looks, just like she used to when I was a kid.

He squints in the twilight but shakes his head.

"Sorry. I don't see anything."

My heart sinks. Am I dying? Has the toxic environment inside the beast poisoned me? Does he not see the giant thing exploding overhead?

I close my eyes, taking in this new information. So, it's real, but no one else can see it. It hurts me, but no one else can feel it. It wants me, and only me.

I open my eyes again, and Toby's eyeballs have disappeared, leaving behind bloody, empty sockets.

I shut my lids again, squeezing them tight. When I open them, he'll be normal. This is a side effect of being in the creature. The toxic sludge is affecting my sensory perception, trying to weaken its prey, that's all. I count silently to three.

I open them.

His face spills over with squirming maggots, the wriggly bugs nestled in the hollowed-out cavities where his eyes should be.

Horrified, I step back, almost losing balance.

Mom's desperate cry pulls my attention.

"Kitty!"

I look at Toby, standing on the bank with the river in the background. Mom on the other side, going quiet as the beast rises high above the water behind him. He stands there, arms at his sides, grinning.

I book it.

As much as I've run in the last week, I have yet to gain any real physical endurance. It's simple fear that pushes me. Where can I go? Somewhere public. A foreign thought, but it never appears in public. The horizon glows with the lights of town. How far is the busy thoroughfare? Could I make it in time?

"Katherine, you can't fight it," Mom calls, her voice in my head somehow. "Don't be like me. Stop running!"

What does she mean by that?

Two balls of light beam directly into my face, blinding me. I shield my eyes as they approach. Headlights. Oncoming car.

Which am I more afraid of? The creature that I know will end my life, or a stranger that only *could* do the same?

In this state, I choose the lesser of my fears.

"Help!" I cry, waving my arms. They have to stop. They've got to see it. I can't be the only one. "Please, help me!"

The car slows, mercifully, and my relief is palpable. The passenger side window rolls down, and the driver leans toward it. He's an older man with a saggy face and kind eyes that don't seem to register my rotten appearance. I catch a glimpse of a hearing aid. "Is everything alright, young lady?"

I shake my head, at a loss for words. What can I say that will make him understand?

"Do you need a ride somewhere?"

Oh, God, do I. I think of the one place it hasn't stalked me. "Can you take me to the hospital?"

He pops the lock, and I swing open the door. I don't think about how I just hailed a random person and voluntarily climb into the car. There are worse things out there than Stranger Danger. "Thank you," I say, buckling up. "Thanks so much."

His nose scrunches. I probably reek of bile and who-knows-what else.

He gives me a curious glance. "You'd rather I call an ambulance? They could help you quicker."

"No, that's okay – thank you."

I just need him to drive. Every second counts.

CHAPTER 28

THE OLD MAN drops me off at the emergency room entrance. I thank him again, letting him believe I'm going in for some much-needed medical attention. But that's not why I'm here – at least not yet – I need to see Mom first.

Keeping my head down, I fight my limp as much as possible to not draw attention. I let my hair cover my face, though the wispy strands feel like a hot fork scraping my blistered profile. I'd glimpsed myself in the old man's side-view mirror; whatever treatment I'd been given was absolutely destroyed by the creature's stomach acid. I'm a walking Halloween monster, pockets of glistening red muscle peeking through my melted flesh, exposed to the world. The pain is ungodly, and I occasionally stop to breathe through it, though breathing does nothing to help. My nerve endings are electrified, sparking misery through my whole body. I'm aware how awful I must look, but I'm hoping everyone'll be too busy to notice. To think I was sneaking out of here not that long ago. Now I'm sneaking back...in even worse shape.

I manage to get to the elevators undeterred, thank God.

In the lift, I take a moment and slump against the wall. The adrenaline has worn off, leaving me exhausted and completely wiped from the ordeal. I'm dizzy and a headache forms behind my eyes as pressure builds inside my skull. I'm thirsty, dehydrated, my mouth dry and papery as I smack my lips to relieve the irritating sensation. It doesn't work.

My belly swoops and drops as I'm carried to Mom's floor, a strange feeling, the cherry on top of this sensory nightmare.

I approach the security desk at the entrance of the ICU.

"I'm here to see Marybeth Hoffman," I say, trying not to wince. Speaking hurts, just like everything else. "I'm her daughter."

The woman behind the desk doesn't look up as she types on a keyboard. "I.D., please. Your name?"

"Katherine Hoffman. But I, uh, don't have identification on me. Forgot it at home. Sorry."

I tap my finger nervously on the counter as she searches for information on the computer.

Her expression softens as she finally looks up. "She's not here, anyway," she says.

What? Where is she? Did they move her to another room, on a different floor? Is she out of danger? Or did they release her home? Oh, God, is she there now, waiting for me?

"Did the doctor not speak with you?" she asks.

"No. Why?"

She hesitates.

"You should really speak with the doctor. Let me see if I can call him for you."

"Can't you just tell me? What is it? Please?"

Her eyes flick between the computer and me.

"It's not my place to –"

"Please."

"Sorry, legally I cannot. I've already said too much. I'm sorry."

If she won't tell me, I'll find out for myself. I'll find Mom, and she can tell me in her own words how she's doing. I back away from the counter and turn around.

That's when I see him coming down the corridor.

"Dad," I mumble.

"Thought you might be here. You left your phone at the apartment again, so I couldn't reach you." He leans in for a hug but pauses, looking me up and down, assessing my wet, sticky appearance. He pulls back, face twisted in distress. "Shit, Kit. You're hurt. What the hell happened? Be straight with me."

I try to explain, but it comes out as stuttering nonsense. He holds up a hand.

"Shh, shh. Never mind. You need a doctor. Oh, my God, Katherine."

His eyes are red-rimmed. He's been crying.

"They won't tell me where Mom is," I say.

"Don't worry about her right now. Let's get you seen."

"No."

"Katherine. Come on." He reaches for my arm but thinks better of it, scrunching his brow. "The faster we get downstairs the sooner they can fix you."

I bark a laugh. Fix me? I'm beyond fixing now. However, that's not my biggest concern.

"I'm not going anywhere until you tell me where Mom is."

He raises his hands in a helpless shrug, looking around as if seeking the aid of a passerby. But the hall is empty. He growls a sigh and rubs his face. I wonder if his five o'clock shadow feels prickly.

"Please," he says, the word muffled in his palms. "Let's just go."

"No." I feel like a toddler throwing a tantrum. If I could, I'd cross my arms tightly against my chest and shake my head. I can't remember what it feels like to move so freely. "Tell me first."

"Well..." He sniffles, loudly, and lifts his gaze to the ceiling. He won't look me in the eyes, and I know what he's going to say before he says it. "I'm so, so sorry to have to tell you, Kit. She passed this afternoon."

Despite knowing it was coming, the news still gut-punches me, and I can't breathe.

"I thought the surgery worked?"

"Any surgery, even ones that aren't high-risk – which she was – there's always a chance."

He touches my arm, and all the pain rushes to the surface. My face screws up in a useless attempt to fight it off. He looks horrified. "Sorry, I'm so sorry."

I don't know if he means for touching me or for Mom.

I shake my head, unable to speak. My teeth grind against both the physical pain as well as this new stab in my heart. I turn away but find I can't take another step. My limbs weaken, and I sink into a puddle on the cold linoleum.

Mom.

My eyes blur with salty tears that sting my face.

"No, no," Dad murmurs, bending close. "Not now. You need to get checked over. She'd want you to get help."

He's right, of course. But what's the point? I should've let the thing digest me while it had the chance. It can't be any worse than this new reality I'm living in.

He takes me down to the ER again, checks me in, and sits next to me while we wait for assistance. We don't speak. We don't make a sound, other than the odd sniffle that he tries covering up with a cough into his elbow, but I catch him wiping his eyes with his sleeve. His knee bounces up and down nervously. But I can't focus on him right now. I stay numb. It's the only way I can get through the repair of my injuries. How we'll mend my heart, that's a whole other question I don't have the ability to answer.

CHAPTER 29

I DIDN'T REALIZE when I walked into the hospital that it would be days before I'd walk back out again. The creature's stomach acid burned away any evidence of my previous surgeries, so I had another emergency round of treatments for the damage, with more to follow. It's grueling, and the torturous pain of the grafting is unbearable. The antibiotics they drip into my bloodstream make me sick, ironically, and the thought of enduring more of this is dreadful.

I don't care. Without Mom, none of it matters.

———————

Five days later, I'm allowed to go home. By home, they mean Dad's apartment. I don't know what'll happen to the house with Mom gone. I can't imagine Dad will want to move back in there, with all the old memories. It'll probably get sold. The thought crushes me.

I think about what happened with the creature. Why did it act like that on the bridge? It had its moment to attack but waited until I fell. Why? And what about Mom? Was she real? If she had already passed by that time, was it her spirit that came to save me? That might explain her voice inside my head – my heart – my soul.

And Toby. I shudder, recalling the way his face transformed, the maggots falling from his eyes. If Mom's spirit was there, does that mean Toby was too? Possessed by the darkness, used as a puppet to get me? If so, I don't know how I can ever look him in the eye again. I've tried calling him, but it goes straight to voicemail. Part of me is relieved. There aren't enough words to formulate an apology worthy of that horrendous experience, and it was all my fault.

I'm on the couch, half-heartedly scrolling through apartment listings. Dad wants to find a two-bedroom for us, and armed with his budget, I'm given the task of seeking out ones I like. It's a mindless activity – I don't care about any of them. They won't be home to me.

I'm interrupted by the sound of squelching, and I freeze. My chest heats with the rapid thumping of my heart. I didn't blink at the hospital, but I'd be lying if I said I wasn't terrified of it happening again. A demented version of the movie *Groundhog Day*, which Dad put on for us to watch this morning. Will it never end? What do I have to do to make it stop?

I whip my head around, scanning the room for the source of the noise. In the corner of my eye, I catch a glimpse of movement, low to the ground. Something darts from beneath the coffee table to the far side of the couch, just out of sight. I pull my knees in close. My lips part, ready to scream.

Something white, no more than a foot wide, rounded and smooth, rises above the arm, stopping when two dark, beady eyes lock onto mine across the upholstered leather. Its ridged body reflects a clear, damp slime in the sunlight.

It doesn't move. It doesn't blink. If it had a nose, it would likely be resting on the couch arm. I'm reminded of a child playing peek-a-boo, but frozen in time.

A maggot on steroids?

We stare at each other. I wonder if it has a mouth, hidden by the couch, that will open wide and take over its entire face.

"What are you waiting for?" I whisper, bitterness tightening my taste buds.

It ripples in response, then stills. Did it understand me?

"What? What do you want?"

Slowly, it rises higher until it's level with me. But it doesn't attack. I shift back, tilting my head to look at it. It watches me with an intensity that sends nauseating shivers deep beneath my healing flesh. The darkness of its eyes swirl with...what? Anticipation? Frustration?

Is this a separate part of the creature? Has it possessed a maggot and shape-shifted with it the way it might've done with Toby?

Feeling vulnerable beneath its gaze, I slide one leg to the floor, followed by the other. My heart tingles with anticipation as I stand, bringing myself to full height. It rises again to match my eye level. A fluttering in my stomach signals a vomiting spell, but I push it aside. It doesn't matter.

Hesitant, I take a step. My mouth dries out as I watch it wriggle, wave-like, in response. It still doesn't come closer.

I step forward again, slowly closing the distance, while every cell of my body screams to flee. I fight that urge, determined to finish this once and for all.

"What are you?" I ask. "How did you find me?"

Fingers trembling, I raise my hand. Inches from its body, I pause. I sense a warm, rhythmic thumping coming from it, almost like a heartbeat. Is it more than just a nightmare? The weight of its gaze suggests a sentient being.

I tilt my head as I watch it watching me.

My hand reaches forward again, almost against my will. Some sick part of me wants this. To touch it, to know how it feels beneath my palm. Will it be cold and slimy? Or surprisingly warm? It does nothing to stop me.

When my fingertips brush its belly, it ripples again, but I can't tell if it's in pleasure or disgust. I run my hand down its body, feeling the ridges. It's a smooth sensation, devoid of temperature. The vibration becomes a long trill. A purr. The flutters in my stomach reach their peak. Laughter bubbles inside me, rising up my throat, and I press my lips together to keep it from escaping.

A slit forms beneath its eyes, a mouth finally appearing. It yawns to the floor, a wet, black hole, the same one that's been taunting me for weeks. My lips that curved into a smile drop back into a frown.

The mouth is nothing but endless darkness framed by teeth. I remember the feel of those tiny, pointed bones. I pull back.

"Hey, Kit." A voice, muted, calls to me from deep inside the creature. It sounds male. It sounds like Toby. "Come here."

I shake my head.

"The water's warm!"

No, no, he's not in there. He can't be. This is a trick. I grab my head and step back, catching the back of my knee on the coffee table. I stumble. The creature still doesn't move.

Toby calls my name repeatedly, like a skipping record. *"Kit. Kit. Kit."*

I kneel. My head hangs heavy. It's an illusion. The creature's manipulating me again.

Or is it?

It hasn't made a definitive attack. It only follows me home. When it swallowed me, it saved me from hitting the river. In some imperfect way, it saved my life. Maybe it can't help that its teeth are so sharp, that its stomach did what stomachs are meant to do. The same way I can't help my freckles or my curly hair or my dislike of broccoli. It's just here, existing on this planet, like me.

Have I gone about this all wrong? Has it been...trying to *help* me?

"You wanted me out of the house," I whisper. "You tried scaring me out with the bugs and the glitchy TVs and the face in the polish. You made me blink when I was vulnerable. You put me in those scary situations. Why? To prove something?"

I survived all of it. Was that the lesson? That I'm stronger now for facing my fears? Bullshit. My body is weaker than ever before, my mind more broken. That's the only explanation I have for my calm demeanor in the face of this monster.

Its jaw closes halfway and then fully opens again. An invitation. It's not forcing me this time, it's asking.

I stand again. Bravery, for once, fuels my limbs rather than fear.

I reach for it once more. Stroking its side, it purrs again, and I lean into the vibration. Lifting one leg, I step into the mouth.

———

I don't fight it. I don't claw my way out. Bypassing the initial, acidic sting of entry into its body, I'm rewarded for my courage. My fears soften, and my anxieties liquefy. All memories of break-ins, accidents, and death evaporate from my body, disappearing into the darkness of this cocoon. That relaxed, floaty sensation takes over, and my cells dissolve. The purring hum, not unlike low thunder during a summer's night, penetrates my bones, absorbing the deepest matter inside me like a sponge.

I feel light and free. I've been here before, chasing this sensation. But now I finally grasp it, here in the belly of what I thought was my enemy.

There's no sense of time or space as we merge into one.

I am reborn.

———

I awake on the floor, cheek smushed into the crook of my arm. My lips smack, craving moisture. Slowly, I sit upright, taking in my surroundings. I'm alone in Dad's living room. There's no sign of maggots or creatures.

But there is an absence of something – pain. Peeling back the bandages reveals fresh skin, shiny and pink. I press on it, gingerly at first, then harder, leaving white fingerprints that fade to a normal, healthy color. No evidence of the trauma the last month or so has put me through. My wounds are healed, my body restored. Whatever happened inside the creature put my injuries right. I am transformed, a person anew.

I am whole.

A week later, Dad lets me visit Janelle.

She's awake but not entirely with it. I guess all that time under can make a body weak. Her family brought her home to recover, and I'm nervous about going over there, especially after everything that happened with Toby. I'm not even sure I understand it myself. He hasn't been answering my calls. It just doesn't make sense. Where did he go? I haven't heard from him since that night, the night on the bridge, the night he changed.

Dad drives me to her house. I grip the seat belt the entire time but don't say anything. The fear that once had a chokehold on me has lessened, and I'm able to somewhat enjoy the ride, which is a new, weird experience.

Her neighborhood is larger than mine, with spacious lawns covered in dried, parchment paper leaves dropped by huge, gnarled oak trees. The houses are made of aged brick and crumbling mortar, the sort of home you'd easily imagine being haunted by the ghosts of the '80s.

When I peek in her room, she's in the middle of a game. She pauses it when she sees me, removing her headset.

"Hi," I say. I cling to the doorframe, ready to bolt if necessary. I take in the burnt-orange floral wallpaper in her room that she's clearly tried covering up with numerous black-and-white band posters, mostly rock artists I've never heard of, captured with guitars mid-strum. Her desk setup is far more impressive than mine, with double monitors and an ergonomic gaming chair that looks oh-so-comfy. A huge stack of empty Coke cans line her wall like an art installation, each one turned precisely so the white curly font peeks out from the side. I've seen her room before, in the background of our calls, but in person there are details I never would've known. Residual incense smoke, earthy and sweet, wafts from her velvet pinstripe curtains, and candy wrappers litter the floor next to her bed, mingling with cat hair. I forgot she has a cat, and I'm reminded of the animal we nearly hit. But that feline was black, and I believe Janelle's fur baby is a brown tabby.

Janelle smiles, and that bolsters my confidence enough to come fully into the room. "Hey, you."

Her smile fades like dissolving sugar. "What the fuck, Kit? How did I get knocked out for weeks, but you come out of the accident looking flawless?"

Self-conscious, I tuck my hair behind my ear, aware that my skin has healed perfectly. No scars or blemishes, not even a simple zit on my chin. It's never been this smooth, and I have no explanation for it.

"Not that I'm not happy you're okay," she quickly corrects, and opens her arms for a hug.

I lean into her embrace – it's the second time we've touched like this, and it feels nice. "It wasn't all sunshine and roses," I tell her. "Trust me."

"What do you mean?"

She pulls back and examines me, eyes flitting up and down my body. "Did you get hurt? Are you okay? Oh God, is it something internal? I am so sorry, Kit. Fuck, it's all my fault."

"No. No, it wasn't. This was something else."

Her eyebrow, currently naked of its piercing, raises in a silent question.

How do I tell her? She'll think I'm crazy. What's crazy is wishing I still had the scars as some sort of proof.

I start at the beginning, about the first time I woke up outside. To her credit, she doesn't laugh in my face. But when I get to the part about the experiments, I clam up. How do I explain to her about Toby? She might not take it well.

"This is kind of awkward," I say. "Just hear me out. Your brother, he..."

"Which one?"

"Huh?"

"Which brother? I have three, you know."

"Oh, uh. Toby."

"You mean Timothy?"

"No, Toby," I say, gesturing with my hand. "The male version of you? Your twin?"

She stares at me, unblinking.

"I don't have a twin."

I bark out a laugh that sounds more like a scoff.

She tilts her head, lips parting curiously.

"Toby." I cross my arms, exasperated. "Come on. Quit playing around."

Her lips curl into a smirk. "You're the one playing."

Does she have amnesia or something? Did the coma leave some sort of memory loss?

"Hang on." She taps on her phone before turning it toward me. A family picture fills the screen. Her parents flank her on either side, grinning proudly at the camera. Towering behind them are three young men – none of whom look like Toby.

"You're pranking me," I say. "He's just not in the picture. One of these guys could be a cousin or something."

She shakes her head.

"He was away at college." My voice takes on a pleading tone. "Things were strained between you. He explained about your...well, your drug use. Your addiction." I cringe, hoping she won't be too mad about it.

"My addiction?" She scrunches her forehead. "I mean, I smoke pot once in a blue moon but only for special occasions. Who doesn't?"

"But he told me all about it."

"He couldn't have, Kit. 'Cause there is no Toby."

I turn cold. What does she mean? Was he not real this whole time? Then who was that guy I allowed in my house, in my *bedroom*, unsupervised in the night?

"Where did you get that idea?" she asks.

I sink onto the edge of the bed, dazed. Was he a complex hallucination brought on by the shadow creature? Or simply a byproduct of my own exhaustion? He felt so real. I think of his hands, warm and solid in mine. There's no way my own brain came up with that.

"Jan," I say, but clam up. I just can't tell her I was tricked by a giant monster.

I burst into tears.

Startled, she moves closer and gently pats my back. "It'll be okay," she says. "Maybe one of my dumb brothers was just messing around with you. Want me to call them in here and tell them off? I'm good at that, you know."

I appreciate her not grilling for more, but that's probably because she's too worn out. It's not fair for me to come here and dump my shit on her like this. She's recovering. Just like Mom was.

A fresh round of tears fall down my face. Why did any of this have to happen?

Janelle makes soft hushing sounds. Guilt eats away at me, a thousand tiny nibbles. She's been in a fucking coma, for God's sake. She slept through a whole chunk of her life. I tamp down the envy before it can take root, because nothing about this should be desirable. *I* should be soothing *her*.

"Never mind," I say, sniffling. I wipe my eyes and compose myself. "Just, never mind."

Dad waited to drive me back home. "Everything good?" he asks as I get in the car. I don't know how to answer. We'll be driving back to his empty apartment when I should be going home to Mom. The last few weeks have been an absolute nightmare, and I can't share that with him, at least not anytime soon. And Toby. How can I tell him that he was simply a hallucination? He wouldn't believe me even if I admitted it out loud.

"She's good." That, at least, is good news. Probably the only good news to come from this whole thing.

CHAPTER 30

I WAKE AGAIN with a reluctant groan, eyes sealed shut by the crust of sleep. I pick at corners of my eyelids, removing the sandiness that gathered in the night, and squint. The sun shines bright through the cracks in the white plastic blinds, leaving a striped pattern of light across the beige rug.

My blinds, my rug. My new room.

A gentle knock at the door. Dad's voice on the other side calls my name. "Kit? You up?"

I raise my head and rub my pillow-creased cheek. I still marvel at the lack of scarring. Where there should be thick, hardened dents and crevices, there's only softness. "Yeah?"

Dad pokes his head through the door. "Hey, kiddo," he says. "Didn't want to wake you, but it's after noon and your appointment's in an hour. I know it's a holiday, but she's opening just for you, and we don't want to be late, you know? This schedule, the routine...it's important."

I drop my head back onto my pillow and speak into the fabric so my voice sounds low and muffled. "Okay. I'm getting up. Thanks."

The door softly clicks shut again, and I groan deep into the pillow. Things have been interesting between us. Dealing with Mom's passing is hard, the hardest thing I've ever done. But I'm getting to know Dad again. Know him better, even. It was awkward at first, getting used to each other's presence, but small talk at mealtimes slowly turned into actual conversations.

Though things have been quiet lately, the horror of October, Halloween, the shadow creature, and the terrors in the night are far from behind me. I get out of bed and rummage in the dresser drawer for some clothes. I get dressed quickly so I have time to eat before my appointment. I don't want to be late. I'm in therapy now, and it's going okay. I begged to do it online, but after the initial "get-to-know-you" call, she insisted that in-person visits are vital to my growth. It's weird leaving the apartment on purpose to sit with a stranger who expects me to share my innermost thoughts and feelings. But she's nice and, most important, patient. I have hope that I'll open up more in the future, but for now, it's a start.

I'll never tell her about blinking out, though. Janelle advised that most people won't accept it as truth, and they'll either brand me as a liar or send me away. I still don't fully understand what happened, or why, but at least the cycle's broken, and for that I'm relieved.

Dad bought me a new wall calendar for Christmas. It has cute puppies on it, and he says maybe we'll get a dog for my birthday this year. I don't know if I'll ever be up for walking a dog out in the world like they need, so only time will tell.

I put it up on the wall next to my new bed in our new, two-bedroom apartment. It doesn't feel like home yet, but it's clean and bright. Dad says I can decorate it however I want, which is generous of him. We've already put a couple of framed photos of Mom by the front door so I can see her face whenever I step out into the world. It wrenches my heart and threatens to send me spiraling in a pit of despair, but I'd rather see her than not.

I flip to the first page, January, and the Labrador puppy

chewing on a black-and-gold party hat brings a little smile to my face. Mom would've loved it.

I made it through another night. That makes sixty-two in a row. I've been keeping track ever since.

I click a pen and cross the box marked 1.

ACKNOWLEDGMENTS

Huge thanks and deep gratitude to the following:

My editor, Kylie Lynne (@kylielynne_edit on Instagram), once again for asking the hard questions that shaped this story into a proper novel.

Cate, for your eyes on the early pages of this book, for your energy, support, and never-ending love for Kit, and most importantly, your friendship.

Julie, for your monthly dose of inspiration and encouragement. Our chats light my creative fire, and I can only hope that I return the favor.

Emilie, Sirrah, and Besu, for your beta reading, truth-telling, and advice.

Rob, for being a Tall Glass of Awesome, thank you for helping me with that massive plot hole; this book wouldn't be here without that conversation over tea and tempura. Thank you for helping me achieve my dream of being a full-time writer.

My parents for always supporting me, even though you don't like spooky stuff and probably won't even read this acknowledgement! Thanks for always believing in me, it means the world.

The online writing community, for always being there, day and night. I am continuously humbled by your support. Writing is, by default, an isolating hobby, so I am eternally grateful for my fellow authors and writers who shine a light in the dark.

Readers like you, thank you, for taking a chance on Kit. Without your enthusiasm for the written word, books wouldn't exist. Feel free to leave a rating and review on the platform of your choice, like Amazon, Goodreads, etc. I'd love to know what you think!

Kitt Creative

Heather lives in a charming but haunted little town in Virginia that's full of ghosts that keep her company and inspire her work. She is a member of the Horror Writers Association and has drafted one novel a year since 2002. When not writing, she can be found buying books faster than she can read them, practicing yoga, or eating her weight in thin crust pizza.

Catch up with her on social media:
@heathermihok

Find out more at www.heathermihok.com